MOLOTOV
E D I T I O N S

THE SYNDICATE

a novel by

Clarence Cooper Jr.

Afterward by Gary Phillips

Molotov Editions
San Francisco, CA

Molotov Editions

5758 Geary Blvd. #221
San Francisco, CA, 94121
www.molotoveditions.com

The Syndicate
Clarence Cooper Jr.

Cover Design: Darcy Fray & Domenic Stansberry
Cover Photo: New York World-Telegram
Interior Design: Domenic Stansberry

Library of Congress Control Number: 2018931362

Trade Paper: ISBN 978-1-948596-04-6

First Edition
7 6 5 4 3 2 1

THE SYNDICATE

One

ANYONE COULD TELL AT FIRST glance that Brace Lilly was a fairy. His smooth skin and neat little lips just didn't sit right on my stomach, and the rest of those goons he had standing around his desk looked just as queer as he did, the only difference being those stiff hunks poking out under the armpits of their dinner jackets.

He waved a delicate hand at me. "Sit down, darling."

I sat, but all the rods made me nervous, and I couldn't see the sense in Lou Pulco sending me all the way to the Coast to play hotsy-totsy with a gay boy.

Lilly slid one long forefinger against the side of his cheek and watched me like I was funny, too, and I started to burn just a trifle.

"All right," I said. "I know where the hell I am and who the hell I'm supposed to see. Now tell me what the hell is going on!"

"I thought you were briefed in New York," Lilly said, smiling at the tone of my voice.

"I was told that my services would be worth ten grand, and for ten grand I don't require much information."

He poked one of his joy boys in the ribs and pointed at me. "Isn't he darling?"

"And I am also Andy Sorrell," I said, "who don't like to play ring-around-the-rosie."

"I think that would be fun," Lilly giggled.

"I think it would be fun to come over there and break your head, too."

All the joy boys clustered around him protectively when I said that.

"I would advise you to keep that joking attitude, Mr. Sorrell," he said icily.

"I'm not joking. If you've heard anything about Andy Sorrell, you know he never jokes."

"I've never heard of you," he said casually. "I was sent a directive by the syndicate which informed me you would be on the way soon and that I should do all in my power to let you in on a few people concerned in the cross."

"So let me in, I'm freezing outside."

Lilly raised his head. "I don't see your hurry."

"And I don't see yours. There's a tight season on hurries this year."

"Are you always this sharp?"

"Only when I shave myself."

He took a long cigarette from a gold holder and got up to walk around where he could face me. "I must say, Mr. Sorrell, that you intrigue me."

"You should catch me when I'm hot—I'd kill you."

He turned away abruptly. "Did Pulco give you a run down?"

I nodded. "Harv Cassiday, Al Benedict and Chess Horvat."

He lit the cigarette and puffed on it reflectively. "Well, I haven't seen Harv in a couple of months. Benedict used to hang around with the shake dancer outside, Tina Meadows. Horvat—about the same as Cassiday. They all just disappeared a few months ago after that bank job in Jersey City."

"Thanks for all the help," I said. "I'd never ask you to throw me a life preserver."

"Listen, Sorrell," Lilly said nervously, "that's really all I know! What the hell, how am I supposed to know something about five hundred grand?"

"How are you?"

"All I know is that these fellows were mainstays in Hollisworth up until a couple of months back. All syndicate boys. Cassiday was with the jukebox co-op, Benedict in cigarettes and Horvat in beer. Why they'd ambush a syndicate caper is something I can't understand!"

"It's not so hard when you consider."

"Consider what?"

"Five hundred and sixty grand," I said. "The best understanding in the world."

I stood up, and all those sissies cringed when they actually saw how far I was up. "This shake dancer, tell her to shake her ass out front after the next performance."

Lilly went over to a bar in the rear of the office. "Care for a drink, Mr. Sorrell?"

"When I care for it." I went over to the door. "Right now, I want you to take care of business."

His manner grew cool again, like I'd insulted him. "Are you actually, really, really, a torpedo, Mr. Sorrell?"

"In the flesh," I said, my hands itching to get at him.

Then I went out to the club's lounge, where the air felt a bit cleaner.

Two

TALK ABOUT A LUSH JOINT, Lilly's was the most. That was the name of it, Lilly's. It was about 300 miles from L. A., in the choicest part of Gold Coast country.

I used to live on the sea, long ago. My pop used to take me out on a trawler when I was just a baby; I can still remember it. That was a long time ago, and it was just Pop, never anyone else. Like I was something dirty no woman would own.

Lilly's had that sea flavor, that taste of salt air, a sultry place where the Hollywood jills and juniors could have a few for the road—the back road, where Lilly had several wall-to-wall carpeted cabins for those who found the journey home too long and arduous.

Class, the kind of class I'd been rubbing my hands for all my life.

The band wasn't big, but it had a big band sound, and when the shake dancer Tina showed up in a silver mesh leotard, it seemed as though the roof was caving in.

I've seen shake dancers before, but this gal was something else. She didn't move—her body did. It scintillated under the mesh like a thousand angry glowworms, and when she crawled out of the thing the smooth skin above the wide expanse of her hips wiggled in two parts, disassociated from her spine, it seemed.

Her body reminded me of Carolyn, sleek Carolyn, her twisting thighs and big soft breasts, a thousand years ago, forever, before she died with my baby.

By the time Tina ended her dance, I was clutching her hard to me, my breath short, my fists doubled up into two big clubs, the nails biting into the pits of each hand.

Without concentrating, I could practically feel her body hot and alive in my hands while she stood thirty feet away.

Then she vanished, and I was left with that crazy, crazy, feeling again, getting scared, getting more scared by the day, and what the hell for?

I came down, like a junkie, snatching up presence enough to notice that even the waiter who brought me a double rye looked and acted like a fairy.

I didn't notice when she came, being wrapped up in a thought wave of nothing.

"Hello," she said, sitting down, but she wasn't smiling. She still had her make-up on, eyebrows arching cat-like over faint blue eyes, the lips big and red and ripe-looking. She had gotten into a dressing gown.

"Hello," I said.

"I understand you want to see me."

"That's right."

"Well . . .?"

"I'm seeing you."

"Look, mister," she said peevishly, "I'm in no mood to play games."

"Neither am I."

"Then what the hell do you want?"

"I want you to tell me where I can find Al Benedict."

Her expression never changed. "And why should I tell you where he is?"

"Because I asked you."

"And just who the hell are you?"

"A man who wants to find Al Benedict."

She detected the seriousness in this last statement and looked down at the table to keep from betraying herself. "I haven't seen Al in months."

"That's not what I heard."

"I don't care what you heard!"

"You listen, you big-mouthed broad," I said softly, seeing the look of fear on her face when I took her hand in mine, "you're gonna talk yourself right into a nice, deep hole. You know where Benedict is, you tell me, or you're gonna wake up mighty sorry tomorrow."

That's when the little fella in the pumpernickel pastel came over and tapped me on the shoulder. "Pardon me, sir, but you're disturbing the other customers."

I would have crushed the guy but he was so little, and the wild mop of gray hair wasn't there on his head for kicks.

"Why don't you blow?" I said.

"I'd be most happy to, sir," he said indulgently, "but it's my job to see that everything goes smoothly here."

"How would you like to go smoothly, like butter?"

"I beg your pardon?"

"If you don't get the hell away from here I'm going to roll you up like a piece of Kleenex, friend."

The little guy saw I wasn't kidding and hustled right out of there, and when I turned to Tina again she was looking at me disgustedly.

"I wish all the people like you were dead," she said earnestly. "I know what you are and all the rest of them. I tried to tell Al that you were rotten, all of you! And now you want me to lead you to him, so you can kill him. But you're late, muscleman, oh, you're so late!"

She stood and whirled the gown around her, leaving before I could get out another word.

Her so closely resembling Carolyn, that's what got me. She had no right to look just like her, or to say those things like Carolyn might have said! No right!

I got up and followed her back to her dressing room, but when I tried the door it was locked.

I stood there, watching that door, boiling inside and tasting my own bile green and sour in my mouth. I waited a thousand years for that dame, and when she came out, I exploded. I grabbed her, and she was soft and bending, like a willow reed, like Carolyn, and her mouth was saying dirty things to me with its cleanness.

I dragged her to the back door and out into the darkness of the field behind the club. I started to hit her with my open hand, and then the heat got too much and I struck her with my fist, again, again, seeing the blood spurt from her nose and the soft flesh puff up instantly beneath her eyes.

When I stopped, I was sweating and trembling. She lay between my legs, her dress pulled across the thickness of her thighs, her breasts heaving torturedly.

I reached down and dragged her face up to mine.

"Stop . . ." she said, gasping, "stop . . . no more . . . I'll tell you where Al is, muscleman . . ."

Three

HOLLISWORTH IS NO BURG; IT'S a solid little city, with the exception that it belongs to the syndicate, lock, stock and barrel.

It has a roller rink, city hall and PTA setup, but it also has gambling, dope from the sea and four efficiently-run whore houses. There was no discord and no hue and cry from the citizens, because those individuals who remained healthy in Hollisworth didn't make it any different.

Lou Pulco told me that I could consider the town mine when I arrived, and he wasn't far from wrong. On arrival, I was met at the airport by the manager of the Hollitop Terraces and given a suite on the twelfth floor.

Everything was lavish and class, nothing like those two grand bumps, where I had to give up maybe fifteen hundred to keep the cops off my back after the rub was over. This was my big chance.

Lou had given me a down payment of twenty-five hundred, with seventy-five on delivery, and, brother, I had a lot of things mapped out for that ten grand.

The money, that's what was so important now! After leaving Tina at Lilly's, I went back to the Hollitop to pick up my equipment, a .32 automatic, thinking of Benedict, the first of three parts.

From upstairs I had the desk clerk call up one of those auto rental services, and by the time I got downstairs some little jerk was just pulling up front in a black Impala.

"How far's Blue Haven from here?" I asked him.

"The sanitarium?"

"Yeah."

"Let's see. Go north about ten miles and turn right on 43, the intersection. Can't miss it. It's the first forest you get to, right in the middle. Just keep going until you see a bunch of trees, that's Blue Haven."

"Thanks."

"Hey, mister, you're not going there to visit someone, are you?"

"What business is it of yours, punk?"

"None, mister. I just meant that it's almost twelve-thirty. Visiting hours are over at Blue Haven at nine p.m."

"Thanks."

I drove off in the direction he indicated. It didn't make much difference whether visiting hours were over or not. I wanted to know if Benedict was there, if he actually had the nerve to come back, to be so close, to Hollisworth.

I also wanted to know whether Tina Meadows was lying. It didn't make too much difference, but I wanted to see about her, her closeness to Carolyn. It was crazy, crazy, but I just wanted to see. I felt sorry about hurting her, but I wanted to see if I was right.

I drove for about fifteen minutes, the countryside and the edge of the sea luminously dark, sparkling around the borders like currents of electricity.

When I made the right on 43, I could see the cluster of trees the boy had told me about in the distance. When I pulled up, I had to get out and open the gates of the joint myself. A whitewashed drive twisted through a valley of willows to a large white centerpiece, with a flying white marble cherub, and sitting smack in back of it was the main building, with a garish neon sign as big as any I've seen in Vegas.

I pulled the Chevvy around in front and got out. The doors were revolving, even, and the reception chamber was as big as the lunch room in Grand Central. Subdued fluorescents peeked over the ceiling's ledge, and the lights bounced off the face of the cute little blonde behind the switchboard just right.

"Good morning, sir."

"Good morning."

"May I help you?" She smiled, and I had that feeling again. Why the hell did every woman look like Carolyn to me now?

"I'm looking for a Mr. Al Benedict."

She got up and switched her wide ass around to the register. "I'm sorry, sir, but I see no Al Benedict listed. Could it be another name?"

"Could be."

"Did you want to leave something? We have no visitors after nine p.m., you know."

"A friend told me he was here," I said. "He's the kind of guy who doesn't like to leave his real name when something's wrong with him. I'm sure he's here under another name."

"I'm sorry, sir, but I can't find a Benedict anywhere in our records." She flickered her big eyes at me. "Are you sure that's who you want?"

"Positive," I said, almost convinced that Tina had given me a bum lead. Then I had an idea. "What about a Meadows? Do you have a Meadows listed?"

She flipped through the files again. "Yes sir. In 309. Mr. Charles Meadows, entered by a Mrs. Tenna Meadows."

"Tina?"

"No sir. Tenna. T-e-n-n-a. Would that be the person you're looking for?"

"Possibly. You say he's in room 309?"

"Yes sir. But you wouldn't be able to visit him until later today. One o'clock is our first visiting hour."

"Thanks very much. I'll come back."

I started out, but there was something about her, her body and eyes, that made me come back.

"You must get pretty lonely here on nights," I said.

She smiled up at me shyly. "Sometimes it gets pretty monotonous, I must admit."

"Nobody here but you?"

"No sir. We have a full staff on nights. An intern is usually on duty here in front, but it's coffee break time right now."

That was convenient for me. "Thanks," I said and went out. I took the Chevvy down the road toward the gate about two hundred yards, got out and came back.

The sanitarium was a modernized Elizabethan structure, with a broad conical on the fifth and final floor. I went around to the side and found just what I was looking for, the fire escape. I pulled the ladder down and went up quickly to the third floor, where the escape exit was a window leading into the main hall.

I crawled in and went down the hall until I found room 309. I took the .32 out of my breast pocket and tried the lock. The door was open. I slipped in noiselessly. The lights were out and the only illumination was the starlight spray from the night sky.

In one corner was the bed. I went over and found the night lamp.

The light that washed across the bed shocked the occupant to wakefulness. Blood-reddened eyes swept over me frantically, and I could see the fear. I knew this was Al Benedict.

"Please . . ." he said hoarsely.

"How are you, Al?" I said.

"Don't . . ."

"Lou Pulco told me to come around and look in on you." I took the .32 and put it on a level with his eyes.

"The money," he said, clutching at my sleeve. "I . . . I don't know where . . . I don't know where . . . I'm dying . . ."

"Where's Harv Cassiday?" I said. "And Chess Horvat?"

"Don't know . . . believe me, I don't know! Never seen a dime of the money!"

"You know why you gotta die, Al?" I said softly. "You and Cassiday and Horvat did something the big man don't like, plus he don't like people cracking his private safe. He's mighty angry about that. He wants to know how you three guys got those plans. He wants to know where the dough is. And he wants you dead . . ."

"Please," he croaked, "I'm dying! Cancer of the lungs . . . gonna die, anyway!"

"Where's Cassiday and Horvat?"

"Don't know, swear I don't know! Cassiday . . . came to me . . . told me about job . . . didn't see Horvat till last day. We all split up . . .

payoff in Hollisworth two months ago. It was a cross . . . never seen a dime of money . . ."

"That's too bad," I said.

"Please . . ."

"That's really too bad, Al."

I went over and flicked out the lamp. When I came back I could hear his frightened breathing. I put the .32 in my pocket and made my hands go toward the sound of his breathing until they touched his clammy flesh, his throat, then I began to squeeze, harder and harder, ending the first of three parts . . .

Four

I WENT DOWN TO THE sea after that. I don't know why, I just did. I felt good all over after what I did to him. I felt especially good because Benedict reminded me of a guy I used to know a long time ago, a brain doctor on Ellis Island.

I was hooked for some caper then, I don't know what, but I wasn't much more than a kid.

"Have you ever had nasty thoughts about your mother?" this brain doctor asked me, and I got so goddamn mad I didn't stop until I had my thumbs hooked up in his nostrils and he was screaming murder.

Those saps! They really thought I was nuts after that. But it wasn't that. It was the money, wasn't it? Money was all there was to depend on; it was like going to bed with a woman. You never got tired of it. The money, the money.

"I don't know why I love you, Andy," Carolyn's voice said from the sea, and it was almost like she was sitting right there in the car with me. "You're horrid and brutal and a murderer. You're killing more than one person when you kill, don't you realize that? You're trying to kill that thing within you!"

"And you died," I said, clenching my fists and screaming at the sea. "You dirty bitch, you went and died on me!"

I got out of the car and ran down to the edge of the water.

I shook my fists at the sea. "You don't come back! You come back and I'll kill you again! I'll kill you again!"

It was morning when I got back to Hollisworth. The only thing moving was an old intercity bus. My watch said 3:30, but it had stopped somewhere along the line.

It was funny, but I wasn't tired when I pulled up at the Hollitop's parking area. All day on the plane from New York the day before, then all night last night. I just felt empty, that's all, without any thoughts of today or tomorrow.

I got out and went in. The elevator operator must have been asleep on nine because I rang the buzzer for a full ten minutes before he arrived, a little freckled-faced kid.

"Oh!'" he said, as though surprised. "I didn't keep you waiting, did I, sir? The signal button is out of order."

"Put me on twelve," I said, stepping in.

He shut the doors. "Twelve seems to be a busy floor this morning."

"Yeah?"

"Yeah. Must be something going on. A couple coppers just went up a few minutes ago."

"Cops?"

"Captain Markle and that Hendricks guy. They went up to twelve not ten minutes ago. If you ask me, I bet they got the key to some-body's room."

"These guys come in here much?" I asked cautiously.

"Only when there's some money to be made, like a crap game or yard party, where they can get the goods on some good-body who shouldn't be doing what he's doing."

The elevator whirred to a stop. "Your floor, mister."

"Thanks."

I got out and went down to my room. I had an idea that the two fellows in question had come up to have a chat with me, and even if this was a syndicate town I didn't like cops.

I took the .32 out and punched the button at my door.

It was a short, straw-haired guy who answered, and he must have thought I was Western Union or something because he dropped a jaw screw loose when he saw the heater.

"Hello," I said. "May I come in?"

"By all means," the guy said, throwing the door back.

I shoved the .32 under his heart and gave him a pat on the head. "Where's your buddy?"

"In the kitchen," he said, tight-lipped.

"Call him."

"Vin," he said. "Vin, come out here a minute."

The swinging door to the kitchen swung open and a guy came out, a tall, black-haired guy with a drink of the hostelry's rye in his fist. He was swarthy, with a touch of Italian in him somewhere, and more handsome than I could imagine any cop.

"You must be Sorrell," he said.

"The same."

"Why don't you get out of Hendrick's ass pocket and put that thing away. I'm sure you're aware that we're playing ball for the same people."

"I don't know how sure I am."

Markle went over and sat down on the sectional. "There's need for you to think otherwise. I got a telegram from Lou Pulco yesterday."

"How is he?"

"Fine. He told me to look after you. He said that you're inclined to be a little hot-headed at times."

"That's Lou, always underestimating me."

Hendricks pecked at my sleeve. "May I sit down, too? If you're as touchy as all that I don't like to be in this hot seat."

"Put your gun away, Sorrell," Markle said. "We just came up for a friendly talk."

"How friendly?"

"That's up to you."

So I put my gun away, just like that, not thinking at all. I saw Markle raise his finger briefly, and in that second Hendricks moved around and sapped me at the base of the neck. I went down, face forward, and all that cushy fur on the floor did little to keep my head from cracking wide open.

Boy, was I a sucker!

I felt Hendricks' hand shoot up under my coat and snatch out the .32.

"You bastard," he said, and kicked me in the chest.

"No, Pete," I could hear Markle's voice say behind me, "he's a sonofabitch!"

All of a sudden it was both their shoes, from the front and back. I doubled up instinctively, but my back was unprotected and Markle's shoe tip cut out a fancy step all along my spine. Pretty soon they got tired, and a good slam under the Adam's apple made me quit caring. They lifted me by both arms and dragged me over to the sectional, where I bled all over the print.

"A tough boy," I could hear Hendricks say somewhere downtown.

"A tough, tough boy," Markle amended, blasting me with his fist until my mouth was a gummy cushion of blood.

I coughed up a mouthful and, just as I expected, they moved away to keep from getting splattered.

"You guys are gonna die," I managed to say.

"Look who's talking!" Hendricks said.

I tried to open my eyes, but the water and mush was too much and I could barely make out their outlines.

"I'm a syndicate boy," I mumbled. "You push me too much, you're gonna die."

A wiry hand fastened itself in my collar. "You know why you're getting pushed, syndicate boy?" It was Markle's voice. "You're getting pushed because you pushed someone you shouldn't have."

"What the hell are you talking about?"

He punched me again. "Tina Meadows . . . Get the point, syndicate boy?" He punched me again, this time harder. "You touch her again and I'll kill you! I don't care what happens, but I'll kill you!"

I laughed, laughed. "Love, thy sting doth fill my heart!"

They knew how to work a guy over. They were specialists. They worked me from head to foot.

I didn't know what time they left.

Five

WHEN I CAME BACK TO this world the afternoon sun had focused from the picture window and was burning the hell out of me where I lay on the floor.

I didn't move for a long time, getting myself together.

Ever thought of how one of those big marlins feels after a hard fight, twisting and straining against the hook in its mouth, finally dragged up exhausted and stupefied with pain to the keel of a boat?

That's how I felt, only twice. I pushed my face into somewhat of its former semblance and staggered to my feet, my eyes straining against the brilliance of the sun.

Those guys didn't know it, but they were dead!

I went to the bathroom and washed some of the mess from my face, then, half-reluctantly, I got into a cold shower and tried to rinse away the bruises that covered my body. It was no use, though. They only got bigger and more painful.

I sunk myself in the Sealy mattress and attempted to sleep, but the network of electronic signals sparking from my belly to chest made me work at it only half-heartedly.

So far, it just seemed like I was going along for the ride. The whole show was beginning to get complex, and for a starter it sure put me in one hell of a shape.

I thought about Benedict. The whole thing had been too easy. Markle and Hendricks must have known he was dead, but they didn't say a thing about it. Of course, they were so busy giving me a work-out it probably slipped their minds.

It was stranger than fiction.

WHEN I WOKE UP, IT was to the tune of the doorbell in high C. The first movement was nerve-shattering, but after a while it seemed as though pain were something I'd been used to all my life.

I got up and drew on my pants. When I got to the door the bell had stopped ringing. I thought about Markle and Hendricks and started looking around the apartment for the .32. It occurred to me that they might have taken it with them, but I finally found it thoughtfully tucked into the breast pocket of my suit coat. I checked the clip and went back over to the door.

"Who is it?" I shouted.

"Naida," a woman's voice said.

"Who?"

"Naida Tomeau. Brace Lilly sent me over to see you."

Lilly? I slung the .32 under my right hip and opened the door with my left hand.

"Hello," she said. She was spraddled-legged, with a round little belly under her sexy suit and a devilish curl around the corners of her mouth as she smiled at me. "I'd like to come in, but there's something about a man with his shirt off that makes me cautious."

"Didn't you notice the gun?" I said.

She giggled. "What can a gun do to you that a man can't?"

"That's something I never thought about."

She slipped past me suddenly into the room. "Well, it's something I've thought about, Mr. Sorrell. A gun is useful only when you want to use it."

"Isn't a man?"

"Men are unpredictable." She went over and stretched out on the sectional, tossing her purse over on the coffee table.

"Make yourself at home," I said, closing the door.

She grinned up at me secretly, and her eyes were big and gray-colored, like the agates I used to shoot with Pop on the beach, where the sand was so thick I thought agates were a useless commodity.

I saw now that a woman's skull displayed them perfectly.

"What are you staring at, Andy, dear?" she said. "Why don't you fix me a drink or something? And why don't you put that gun away? Do I look dangerous?"

"Yeah, you look deadly. And the last time I put my gun away, I got taken around the Maypole, on ball bearings, no less."

She giggled again. "You must have met Markle and Hendricks."

"Does it show, or am I blushing?"

"Now, Andy," she chided, "don't be angry. They just want you to know how much they like you."

"And I like them," I said. "We'd tell the world we're in love, but who'd understand?"

I went back to my room and put on a clean shirt. I could hear her rummaging around in the kitchen with the liquor bottles.

"Don't you have any gin?" she called.

I came back out and pushed open the door to the kitchen, where she stood in the breakfast nook that served as a bar.

"You like gin," I said. "I like rye. But I live here."

"That's not a very sociable attitude," she pouted.

"I'm not a very social kind of guy," I said. "Listen, just what the hell do you want?"

"I told you, Andy! Lilly sent me over."

"And just why would Lilly send you anywhere?"

"Well, Jesus, I'm his wife, aren't I?"

I was shocked, I don't know why. I just never imagined fairies married women.

"I know what you're thinking," she accused, shaking a finger at me like I was a naughty boy. "But you're wrong—it's just like you don't think it is."

"That explains everything," I said.

She brushed past me with a bottle of rye and one of soda and went into the living room, where she spread herself out again all over the furniture. "Bring, a glass with you from the kitchen, won't you, darling? A large one."

I went back and picked up a couple of tumblers.

"Thank you, sweet," she cooed. "Now, after I finish this drink, I'll tell you why I'm here."

"You'll tell me now," I said.

She put her hands up in front of her face in mock protection. "Please don't strike me, Mr. Sorrell!" She patted a spot next to her on the sectional. "Do sit down, darling, and I'll tell you a story."

"I just woke up."

"This is not for bedtime, sweets—it concerns Chess Horvat."

I came over and sat down next to her. "This story is one that might interest me."

"I thought it would," she said, smiling mischievously. "You and I know that Cassiday, Benedict and Horvat got hold of the plans for the bank heist several months ago, executed it and got away with over five hundred grand."

"That's the information I have."

"So much for that," she said. "How they got the plans, no one knows, but it had to be on the inside wire. Benedict is dead—" She chucked me under the chin— "Someone saw to that. He didn't have any part of the cash, but that 60-dollar-a-day fee at the sanitarium was being taken care of somehow."

"So what does that explain?"

"Why, it's simple, darling. One or both of the boys were taking care of the expenses." She poured herself a drink and took a long pull at it before she continued. "Lilly figures that the fellas came back here to split up the money, but something happened and they had to hang around."

I thought about what Benedict had told me about the arrangement for the divvy two months ago.

"What else does Lilly figure?"

"He figures that both boys are in, or around, town. He told me to tell you that Horvat used to hang around with a little rich deb named Meg Inglander. She lives out near Fernando, with her old man. The joint would make an excellent hideout."

I started to get moving, but something made me stop and think.

"Just what is Lilly getting out of this?" I said.

She didn't make a very good try at appearing surprised. "Why, Andy baby, Lil doesn't want anything! He was told to co-operate, you know that."

"Were you told to co-operate, too?"

"I don't get you."

I reached down and unbuttoned her suit coat, ran my fingers up around her firm little breasts, felt the nipples rise in response through the thin cloth of her bra.

"Now do you get me?" I said.

She grinned at me impishly again. "But, darling, we've only just met."

"Can you think of a better way to cement a new friendship?"

She put her glass down and raised up until her lips were on a level with my own. "You're not a bad looking guy, Sorrell, give or take a bruise."

"And you're not a bad-looking dame." I crushed her mouth under mine, tasted it hot and foamy sweet, her breath short and fragrant, like a baby's. It would have been an innocent kiss, except for the way she made her tongue do things.

In my bedroom, she strung it out, like she was experienced in this form of torture. Mischievously, she raised her skirt until I could see her blue silk panties and garter belt, then she slowly drew her nylons from those long, smooth legs. Next came jacket and skirt, blouse, and she paused to watch the hard way I was looking at her.

"Darling!" she said with a gushy, bitchy laugh.

I knew women like her. Even when I started to do the rest of it for her, I knew that was what she wanted, what she had planned from the start. The bra was easy enough to get off, but when I got to the panties she made it purposely hard, twisting her hips on the bed so the silk caught under her weight, pushing the bulk of her thighs against me, hampering me.

She made me use my strength against her, force her, and all the while she was laughing, her voice rising higher with her every subtle resistance.

Finally, I raised her body and snatched the damn things off.

"Oh, Andy," she said in a gusty voice. "Come here, darling Andy!"

The rose hue of her nipples pointed outward to me, like her arms, the trim little naked belly nestled at her thighs, beckoning with satisfaction.

"Be brutal, dear," she said, taking me, and I had a sharp instant of regret. "Burst me, Andy, make me explode!"

The bed received us. I didn't like the way she devoured me; it was the man who was supposed to consume. She drew it out until I felt my bowels were evacuated, then, when she was tired of it all, she siphoned out the very core of my brain.

We lay breathless together.

"That was very good," she breathed against my ear.

"It could have been a helluva lot better," I said, coming out of the spider web grasp of her.

I went back to the bathroom, wondering whether Carolyn had seen any of it from wherever she was.

Right then, I didn't give a damn.

Six

WHEN NAIDA LEFT MY APARTMENT that evening it was damn near time for supper. I went down to the hotel's dining room, but only wound up having a couple of ryes. I was hungry, but it was for something other than food.

The fixer and in-between man for the syndicate, Pulco indicated vaguely that there was little chance of me getting a direct line on that half million. My job, mainly, was to find the parties responsible for the job and give them the rub. If I bumped into the dough along the way, good and well enough, but Pulco hadn't given me any orders for such an occasion.

I began to think about that dough. All that dough. I wasn't to blame if I happened to find it, was I? And five hundred grand made my promised one-fiftieth seem mighty small.

I paid my check and went out to the parking lot. I expected the attendant to do a double take when he saw my kisser, but he acted as though rubber stamp lips and purple eyes weren't a particularly uncommon sight. They probably weren't, in Hollisworth.

I goosed the Chevvy out on the main drag and started for Fernando, after I got my bearings at a filling station.

I'm a sucker to an extent, but after that point my IQ starts to pick up a little. Naida and Lilly had applied the grease to me in more ways than one. Gay boy's motive for providing me with information about the Inglander broad had designs with a dollar sign.

It'd be foolish for me to think that I was the only one hoping I'd stumble over all that green.

I couldn't seem to fit Naida into the scheme of things, nor Vin Markle and his flunky Hendricks. It wasn't hard to surmise that Markle had a crush on the Meadows dame and came after me because of the workout I gave her. Otherwise, that seemed to be the only thing he was concerned about. And being a part of the machine in Hollisworth, he'd naturally heard about Cassiday, Benedict and Horvat.

And Naida, right out of nowhere, here she comes, easy, pliable. With a husband like Lilly, though, a woman couldn't help but be loose.

The evening sun was hiding behind a hilly pass when I noticed the car behind me. It kept a discreet distance but not discreet enough. I speeded up, it speeded up. I slowed down, it slowed down.

I took a cutoff and detoured about five miles until I came back to the highway. I lost the tail. Or at least I thought I lost him. A couple of hundred yards down the road I saw the car parked next to the pump of a filling station. The guy must have known where I was going!

When I drew abreast, the driver tried to hide his face, but I got a good look at him. It was the little guy in the pumpernickel pastel at Lilly's. I kept on down the highway as though I hadn't noticed him.

Lilly seemed to be covering every angle! In the rearview mirror I saw the little guy bounce out on the highway after me. I pushed the Chevvy up to eighty for about twenty seconds and slowed down at the next bend.

A private road angled out onto the highway. I twisted in quickly and paused, making sure that my pumpernickel pal got a good glimmer before I set off down the road in a cloud of dust.

A winding border of eucalyptus made the thing perfect! I stopped abruptly, flipped the selector stick into reverse and let the rear wheels dig me around so that I was horizontal on the road. I got out, plucking the .32 from my breast pocket, and loped over to the driver's side of the road.

The little guy didn't see the Chevvy till the last minute, and by the time he had brought his car to a sliding halt, I had the door on his side open and was practically sitting in his lap, the .32 socketed just under his left ear.

"Please! Please!" he screamed. "Don't kill me!"

I took hold of his tie and dragged him out on the gravel. "I'll make it painless," I said grimly, bending over to plant the gun muzzle dead center on his forehead.

"Don't, don't, Sorrell!" he pleaded. "I'm only doing what I was told!"

"Who told you to do what?"

"Brace Lilly—he told me to follow you. I swear that's all I know! He said just to follow you everywhere you went and then report back to him."

"Aren't you a little old to be playing tag?" I said. "What's your name?"

"George Eversen. I'm the headwaiter at Lilly's. I swear, Sorrell, I don't know what's going on! I get paid good money at Lilly's. There's not much I can refuse to do for him."

"Maybe you get paid well enough to die for him."

The little guy saw I wasn't kidding and started to blubber.

"Please, Sorrell, I know something you don't! It was Lilly! Lilly was the one who arranged to get those bank plans from New York! Lilly set the whole thing up through his associates with the syndicate, that's the truth!"

"A few minutes ago you didn't know a damn thing."

"I hear things, Sorrell! Lilly trusts me!"

I took the .32 away from his skull. "Get up, Pops."

The little guy scrambled to his feet. "You'll never regret this, Sorrell. I'll tell Lilly anything. I'll tell him I lost you on the road."

"Where do you think you're going?"

"What?"

I waved him back with the rod. "You say Lilly arranged to have those plans hijacked in New York, right?"

He wrung his hands nervously. "That's what I heard around the club, Sorrell, I swear to God it is!"

"Where's the dough?"

"What?"

"The half million bucks, stupid! Where's it at? If Lilly arranged to lift all that cash, he must have it around somewhere."

"I don't know, Sorrell. Right after the bank was robbed a few months back, Cassiday and Horvat came to the club to see Lilly. I didn't hear what they said, but I could see they were pretty mad when they came out of the office."

"Was that the last time you saw them?"

"No, I saw Horvat a few days later. Lilly sent me over to his beach house to pick up a case of champagne from the cellar. I came in the back way with a key and I could hear Lilly and Horvat arguing in the dining room. They were saying something about the money, but I didn't get a chance to hear anything definite because they stopped talking when they heard me come in."

"For a guy who don't know nothing, you know a lot," I said. "How does Naida Torneau fit into this thing?"

"It was just a marriage of convenience. They were married about six years ago, when Lilly took over the club. Because he's got a morals record, he couldn't get a license to run the place. Everything is in Naida's name. She was a bum when she married him, Sorrell, nothing but a bum."

I watched him closely. "Say that again." He didn't understand.

"About her being a bum," I said. "Say that again."

"Well, that's all she is, Sorrell!" he said heatedly. "A bum, a tramp!"

Love, thy sting, I thought. Vin Markle wasn't the only guy in Hollisworth with a helluva crush.

I went over and got in the Chevvy, pulled around Eversen's car and pointed my nose toward the highway. I got out and went back over to him.

"I'm gonna give you a job, little fella," I told him. "You're gonna keep your eyes and ears open and every goddamn time Lilly goes to the john, you're gonna rush right over and tell me. Understand?"

"Sure, Sorrell. I don't want any trouble."

"You won't get any if you do exactly as I tell you."

I left him standing there and got back in the Chevvy. When I pulled out on the highway, the sudden pall of night required me to switch on the headlights.

I went down the highway about five hundred yards and waited until I saw the headlights of Eversen's car pull out on the road and swivel around in the opposite direction, then I started off.

Like I said, I'm a sucker, but only just so far. It was hard to believe that Lilly had the money. I didn't think Eversen had lied to me, but it didn't make sense that Lilly should bait me with his wife. You don't bait a hook unless you're trying to catch something, and in this case I thought Lilly was fishing for a prize catch—five hundred grand.

There was another way to think about it, too. It was possible that Lilly wanted to make things as easy as possible for me to collect my ten grand, then he wouldn't have to split all that green with anyone.

If that's the way it was, gay boy had another thought coming.

It was nothing to kill three men for ten grand. I'd kill fifty men for half a million dollars.

Seven

I SAW THE INGLANDER RETREAT while I was still five minutes away. It was shiny and big, on a tall slope with trees, like the calliope I saw one time in a circus my old man took me to, high-reaching Colonial spires that looked like eyes staring off over the black, distant land.

It was like a castle.

"See that?" my old man had said of the big, hooting thing. "That's rare, boy, real rare."

I don't know why the goddamn house looked like a calliope, but it did, and as I drove up the long, twisting drive to the gaping black mouth of the front entrance I expected to hear those big pipes scream off over the world and hear my old man say, "That's rare, boy, real rare."

One pane of glass in the front, almost fifty feet long, let me look in on the cultured expanse of the front room, where bookcases swung around the wall with a thousand teeth. There was a reading lamp burning over the desk, but no one was around.

I struck the chimes with my thumb and watched a slick-faced guy in a black monkey suit and bow tie, through a panel in the front door, march out of a door near the staircase.

"Yes sir?" he said stiffly when he opened the door.

"Is Miss Meg Inglander in?"

"Are you a member of the party, sir? Miss Inglander is entertaining at the pool."

"I'm the party," I said, stepping in. "Where's the pool?"

The guy looked down his nose at me. "Please follow me, sir."

So I followed him through heaven. Wall to wall carpeting? This joint looked as though the walls were even carpeted. When I looked at this rich man's world, my mouth watered.

I thought about that five hundred grand and how much it could do to set me up in this sort of shape.

The guy in the bow tie took me through the kitchen and out a little door that led down a tiled slope. It seemed as though we were going down to the basement, but after a while I saw that the house had been built that way purposely on the flat side of the hill.

In a few seconds I could hear voices and laughter and the sound of strings weaving luxuriously through it all. We came out on what looked to be a patio, but it was bigger than a tennis court.

At the far end was the pool, and guys and dames in swimming suits were lounging around the edge. Occasionally someone would dive in, but it would only be to swim across to the bar, where a waiter stood on call.

The hi-fi, wherever it was, accompanied several swim-suited dancers, and the lighting was obscure, which made the whole thing very cozy.

My escort left and went over to one of the couples. He spoke to a doll with very long but shapely legs. She broke away from her partner and came over toward me. She had those great big luscious breasts, like Carolyn, and the tiger-striped bikini halter was doing all it could to hold them in. The little piece she had knotted around her ass had given up.

She looked up at me inquiringly, and I wondered how Horvat had ever managed to get anything as beautiful as she was.

"May I help you?" she said in modulated tones. "If it's my father you want to see, he's out of town at the moment—Richards should have told you that."

"It's not your father I want to see."

She gave me the once over keenly. "I don't believe I know you, Mr.— "

"I want to talk to you privately," I said.

"I'm very busy now. Couldn't you tell me what it is you want?"

"I want Chess Horvat."

Her expression became very distressed for a moment, and it was all she could do to keep from pushing me into a little study off the side of the pool.

The room was equipped with a divan and bar, which seemed to be a common fixture around the joint.

She went over and got a cigarette out of the pearl box on the table and set fire to it nervously with the matching lighter.

"May I ask why you want Chess, Mr. —— "

"Blow," I said. "Joe Blow."

She took time out to make herself a quick drink. "All right, Mr. Blow, or whoever you are, what do you want with Chess?"

I found a spot on the divan, where I could get a dog's-eye view of her figure. "I want to let him know he's holding a winning ticket in a popularity contest. First prize is a slug in the head."

She slammed her drink down on the bar. "Are you mad?"

"Sometimes I wonder."

"If you've got something to say, say it and get out of here."

"Where's Chess Horvat?"

She crushed her cigarette out in a tray. "Are you from the police?"

"Were you expecting them?"

"Certainly not! It was just your manner—"

"Where's Chess Horvat?" I said again.

She lit another cigarette, took a couple of draws and stubbed it out. "I haven't seen Chess in several months."

"You're lying."

She whirled around angrily. "And just who, may I ask, do you think you are to talk to me that way?"

I got up. I started to burn. I went over, but I didn't touch her. I came over close and stood looking down the deep cleft of her breasts until I thought they'd pop out of that thing with her frantic breathing.

"You know where Horvat is," I said, "and you're going to tell me."

"Please, I don't know where he is!"

"Miss Inglander, you're gonna make me real mad in a minute . . ."

"Please believe me!" she cried, clutching me by both arms. "I haven't seen Chess in two days! He's in some horrible trouble, I just know he is!"

"Then he'll be back here?"

"I don't know!" She looked up at me pleadingly. "Please don't hurt him! He said someone was looking for him, someone wanted to kill him. I'll give you anything you want, only don't do anything to Chess, please!"

She was telling the truth, I could see that easily enough. The fear had her trembling. The desperation in her excited me. If I hadn't held myself, I would have grabbed her. I felt funny again, and I thought about Carolyn. All I could see was those big, motherly breasts and the stiff eyes of the nipples poking out under the stripes, begging me, begging me.

I wanted to touch her, but I knew I'd go crazy if l did. I just stood there, feeling warm below the belly, and I couldn't even think straight. It was the fear in her that did it, and I wanted to squeeze her against me, I wanted to wrap my hands around her big rump and pull her close, tight and close, all the way inside me, like Carolyn.

I couldn't stop thinking like that! Why was it getting worse all the time?

"Please, please, don't hurt Chess!" she was saying. "I'll do anything, but don't hurt Chess!"

I tried to get out of there before I exploded, but I couldn't. All I could see was those big mother breasts bursting out of the tiger stripes, and her wide hips seemed to be wiggling in anguish.

Before I knew it, I had reached out. That crazy thing in me had made me reach out. My fingers clutched down in the bra and it disintegrated in my hands. I heard her voice saying "No! No!" but it was too late then. Her full breasts filled my hands, and her fingernails were digging across my face, trying to find my eyes.

Outside myself, I watched me pick her up and throw her onto the divan; then I saw me snatch that flimsy thing from about her hips. She was all mountains of soft flesh, hairless and virgin-like.

In a trance, wild, crazy, I could hear her sobbing defeatedly as I got out of my clothes. But I wasn't really there, even as I did those things, even as I told myself that I was doing something mad.

I watched her trembling, an arm across her eyes, and I was urged on by her fear. But there was something else, something that made me stand there for a long time and watch her that way, naked, soft, and helpless. Made me stand there building up that perverted lust until it seemed to be coming out of my ears, until it expanded and exploded in me, then finally throw myself on her like a wild animal.

It was quick and sudden and good, and though I knew I received no response from her it felt as though I had swallowed her within myself and my swelling, buoyant tides were her own.

"Even this doesn't matter," she murmured in a dead, vanquished voice.

I lay on her finally, exhausted and somehow ashamed. "Even this doesn't matter," she said again, "for Chess . . ."

When I got out to the Chevvy my heart was going fast and I was sweating. I let the window down out on the highway and the rush of cool air cleared my head, and my mouth felt fuzzy and warm.

I was going crazy . . . crazy, crazy, crazy!

Eight

WHEN I WOKE UP THE NEXT day I didn't remember anything, and it was only after I'd laid there in bed for a long time that I could remember the first little bit of last night's events.

My clothes were tossed all over the room and an empty fifth bottle of rye perched up snugly on the pillow next to my head.

I didn't notice I was naked until I staggered into the bathroom and held my head under the shower. I felt rotten and my hands were shaking like a wino's.

Way back in the rear of my head a little voice was scaring the hell out of me. I started walking around in circles, not knowing what to do first. I went into the living room and pushed open one of the windows, looked down on the little people and the little cars and the whole lousy little world. I felt like getting out on the parapet and taking a nosedive, smashing every goddamn thing there under me.

Pretty soon I was able to pull myself together and call room service for a pot of black coffee. In the meantime, I stood under the cold shower until I felt like a Popsicle, then got into some fresh clothes.

When the coffee arrived, I laced it with a double jigger of rye and swallowed it down before my stomach had a chance to say anything about it. I warmed up a little, and all the marbles started clicking on time.

What was going wrong with me? I held my hands out. They kept trembling. It was getting closer and closer to me, ever since two years ago and Carolyn. Was I really going off my nut?

I stopped thinking about it. I started thinking about that half million again and tried to keep it foremost in my mind.

Horvat had been around Hollisworth as close as two days ago, Meg Inglander had assured me of that. And with Horvat so near at hand, could Cassiday be far behind?

It was a stickler, and with things happening to me the way they were I felt like an invalid in a sea of jelly. Naida Torneau's idea about Horvat and Cassiday having the dough didn't pan out so conveniently now. I couldn't see them hanging around with that much green just to take care of a guy who was going to die, anyway.

This avenue of thought led me back to Brace Lilly. It made sense now. Lilly had the money and was making it as easy as possible for me to pick up the trail to his accomplices.

Yet why would Lilly hang around at all? Five hundred grand could have bought a guy an express ticket to the moon, if he wanted to go that far. And Lilly, even if he decided to stick around and make sure the parties in question were all dead, was taking one helluva chance. You don't dribble out that much money, and someone was sure to notice if he started getting prosperous later on.

There was some other angle to the whole thing, I felt it. Eversen said Lilly had arranged to have the plans swiped by one of his syndicate associates. Did this guy, whoever he was, have the money?

It was a provocative thought but not very progressive. There were very few people in the syndicate who had access to the kind of information that would make such a cross possible.

I went into the bedroom and put on a tie, but the doorbell rang before I had a chance to draw it up. Still mightily impressed with my gentlemen callers of the night before, I got the .32 and went over to the door.

"Who is it?"

"Mr. Sorrell?" A woman's voice.

"Who is it?"

"Meg Inglander. Let me in, please let me in!"

I went over and put the gun under the sectional's pillow. When I came back she was ringing the bell again and she didn't stop until I'd opened the door and snatched her hand away from the eyelet.

"What the hell's wrong with you?" I snapped.

It was acute relief that made her dig a hand into my arm. "Oh, please, please, let me in!"

Behind last night, I had to get acquainted with her face once more. The wide, trembling mouth struck up a vague memory, but it was the fear in those eyes again, that tortured fright, that made me see the same woman under the austere brown ensemble. She couldn't look at me, not after last night.

"Please don't be angry, Mr. Sorrell. I had you followed last night, that's how I knew how to find you."

I stepped aside and let her come in. "What do you want?"

"It's about Chess," she said, turning to me, "but you must promise me you won't do anything to hurt him."

I shut the door and came over to her. "Have you seen the boyfriend?" I felt odd, talking to her this way.

"Please, Mr. Sorrell——" Her eyes sparkled with hate.

"Stop it! You're pleasing me to death. Just tell me where he is."

"He says he knows you're here to kill him," she said haltingly.

"You know where he is, then?"

"Yes, but I can't tell you where until I'm sure you won't hurt him."

I turned away because that frightened thing about her was getting to me again. It wouldn't cost me anything to tell her I wouldn't do anything to Horvat, and I wouldn't—not right away. I wanted to talk to him first.

"Why should Horvat want me anywhere close to him if he knows I'm around to knock him off?" I said.

"He wants to tell you something—he says it's very important."

I can tell you I considered everything backwards and forwards before I told her okay. The whole thing could easily be a trap. Knowing I was on his and Cassiday's tails, Horvat could imagine better places for me to be than walking around out in public with my hot little hand wrapped around a rod—a very deep hole, to name one. Still, if he had the money, it would be just as easy to pay me off.

"Where do we meet the boyfriend?" I said, going for my coat.

"Wait, Mr. Sorrell!"

When I turned, the lady had a big .38 perched in her shaking little fist and it was pointed at me, somewhere around the strike zone. I should have known it was inevitable, but what can I expect of me?

"I could kill you now, Mr. Sorrell," she said softly. "I should—after what you've done to me."

"I won't argue the point."

"You're not going to do anything to Chess," she said firmly, "do you understand that?"

"I'm no dumbbell, but sometimes I wonder."

"Before you see Chess, you must believe that he has no part of that horrible money. If anything happens to him, I swear I'll hunt you down and kill you. I love Chess more than anything. I'd see every person on earth dead just to have him."

She wasn't joking about anything she said, and my stomach began to feel a bit queasy under the line of fire. "Where do we go from here?" I said.

"There's a small art gallery attached to the rear of my home. It's accessible from a back road. Come up at 10:00 tonight. You'll be seen and admitted. And don't come armed, Mr. Sorrell, or Chess'll kill you on the spot."

"I don't like those terms."

"Those are the only terms under which you'll see Chess." She backed toward the door without taking her eyes off me. "And remember what I said. If you so much as touch Chess, I'll kill you."

After she was gone, I went into the kitchen and hit the rye bottle again, hard. It didn't help much.

Whatever the fatal attraction Chess Horvat had for Meg Inglander, it was certainly a strong one, and I didn't intend to fall victim to his charms. I would go to see him tonight, but I'd have on all my clothes, including the .32.

I looked at my watch. 2:25. I had a lengthy waiting period. I went over to the phone and got the broad on information to give me the number of Lilly's joint.

The delicate bruiser who answered the phone told me Mr. Lilly hadn't arrived yet but I could talk to Mr. Eversen, if it was important. It was important and I did want to speak to Mr. Eversen.

"Hello?" the little guy said in a while.

"Sorrell," I said. "You haven't forgotten what I told you yesterday evening."

"Oh, no, Mr. Sorrell! I've been doing exactly as you said, only nothing's happened yet."

"Where's Lilly?"

"He won't be in till later."

"How late?"

"I don't know, Mr. Sorrell. He called from the beach house an hour or so ago and told me he'd be delayed this evening." I hesitated for a moment. "What do you know about a Meg Inglander?"

"Oh, her. Blue book, active in society circles. She used to go with Chess Horvat, did you know? Horvat was the friend of a friend—you understand. They started going around steady about six months ago and her father, Lemuel Inglander, crusty old millionaire, didn't hide his displeasure. They used to come into Hollisworth all the time. The whole town knew about it."

"The young lady made one of her social visits by my place a few minutes ago," I said, "but what she served for tea was a lot more persuasive."

Eversen's voice perked up with interest. "Was it about Horvat?"

"The same. We have a date tonight at her place."

"What do you want me to do, Mr. Sorrell?"

"Nothing right now. I've got a hunch about Lilly. I'll call you back in a little while."

"All right. Anything else?"

"Yeah—keep your mouth shut."

I hung up. Suppose this *was* a trap. I was wondering now.

Oddly enough, Lilly couldn't be reached at the moment, and if the information Eversen had given me about gay boy was on the level,

Lilly and Horvat could very well be composing a funeral march for my benefit.

Only one thing about those sonatas: I don't like them unless they're being played for someone else.

Nine

I LEFT THE HOTEL AT ABOUT 9:00 p.m.

Across the street, at a drugstore counter, a guy was asleep with his face in his hat. He should have kept his hat on. I recognized the straw hair.

I was doing forty coming out of the parking lot, and when I made the main way I was marking time with the stoplights. My tail could never make a professional, because he got chicken too easy.

Out on the highway, I took my time.

It was better this way, just sitting and thinking calmly, and I avoided thoughts of Carolyn just like I avoided the thoughts that brain doctor tried to make me think about my mother a long time ago.

Lou Pulco was probably wondering why I hadn't sent him the okay signal, but he told me the job would unquestionably take a bit a time. What he hadn't figured on was that I'd set my sights on the many monies.

If Lilly and Horvat had arranged a string of funnies, they had a surprise coming, what with my sense of humor. They would be counting on me arriving unarmed and free of suspicions, but I wasn't built that way.

Then I thought about Meg Inglander, and started having doubts again.

There was something about her that had me thinking screwy. If she loved Horvat as much as she claimed, and he really wanted me out of the way, why didn't he have her take care of it? The chance of there being any complications were small, as big as the Hollitop was. And even if there were, the local gendarmeries and I weren't very fond of each other. They would have been glad to whitewash the whole thing.

Here I was again, goofing up the perfect patterns I'd created. There was something about the Inglander dame's plea that was too sincere. On the other hand, she didn't have to know what Lilly and Horvat were planning and could have truthfully thought that things were to be exactly as the boyfriend said they would.

I pulled off the road at the next filling station and looked at my watch. Only 9:30. I went inside the joint and leaned over the Coke machine to get at the wall phone.

When the guy at Lilly's answered this time he told me that Eversen had stepped out for a moment and Lilly hadn't come in yet.

My doubts about Lilly grew a little bigger. I checked myself and got back in the car. It was all rounding out to a neat package. Chances were that Lilly was one of the welcoming committee at a party where I was to be guest of honor.

I started to burn some, and felt glad about the whole thing, kind of.

I was a clay pigeon on the approach.

The road was framed in the light of bush-high kliegs and the ascent was steep. The art gallery poked out like a bent finger at the fringe of the mansion, shyly exposing one darkened window from a shelter of fruit trees.

Over all this was a soot-like darkness which created too many illusions.

I stopped the car a couple of hundred feet from the entrance and got out. The .32 fitted snugly in the palm of my hand and I held the gun arm half-crooked in front of me, where the heater blended in with my suit.

I walked slowly until I came to the edge of light, then danced out of the illumination quickly, making a wide bend to the windowless right panel of the doorway. From this protected position,

I reached around and tapped three times on the heavy facing of the door. No sound came from the interior. I knocked again. Still no answer.

This was something like I'd expected. I reached around cautiously and found the ring latch of the door. I turned the thing slowly until I felt the catch give and the door move back silently a few inches.

I braced myself, put a foot against the door, then shoved.

The darkened inside blazed up suddenly and exploded. A slug whirred itself to a stop in the door facing just over my head. I squatted and pressed the happy button, felt the little machine in my hand buck to life with two brief spurts of fire.

Somebody scrambled across the room and slammed into the wall at the other side. I pointed the mouth of my heater in the direction of the sound and let it cough off three messages deeply.

There was no return fire. I slipped into the room and crouched near the baseboard on the left side of the doorway. No sound. I stood up carefully and ran the edges of my fingertips around the wall until I found the switch. I waited several minutes before I threw the thing on but still didn't get any response.

When the light flushed over everything, I saw that the door on the other side of the room must have delivered my pal with the pistol to the inside of the house.

My immediate surroundings were a jumble of confusion. Statues were broken and paintings knocked from the wall. It looked as though there'd been one hell of a fight.

In the rear another doorway looked like it might be the entrance to a storage room. I went over and gave it a shove with the tip of my shoe.

The first thing I saw was his feet. In the half-light, the little room looked like an artist's workshop, with one huge, clay-ragged table.

He looked as though he'd been dragged under the table. When I bent down I could detect a slight breath, and when I turned the guy over he started throwing up a sweet-smelling greenness from his nose, making the virile young mustache on his top lip look like a dead piece of shrubbery. There was the slight smell of hand lotion that reminded me of the Jergens product.

His eyes parted stickily and swung up vaguely until they settled on my face.

"Horvat," I said, dragging him up by the shirt. "You're Horvat, aren't you?"

He understood that much and shook his head weakly. "The money," I said, my voice steady, "where's that money, Horvat?"

Another gush of that sweet-smelling puke was his only answer. A frame-jarring shudder passed over him. He stiffened suddenly, then became limp in my hands. The eyes stayed open and blank.

I dropped him on the floor and stood.

The whole goddamn thing was getting mucky. I recognized poisoning when I saw it.

Ten

I HEARD SOMETHING ALMOST LIKE the scratching of mice just as I was about to get out of there. It came from around the other end of the table where a leg shield hid the back wall from me.

I hoisted my rod over the ledge and circled around the far end.

What I saw was far from being a mouse or anything related; it was Meg Inglander, and the back of her pretty head was one big grapefruit sop of blood. Someone had sapped her and they hadn't cared how hard they did it.

It was the sound of her fingernails against the hardwood floor that had gained my attention. Half conscious, she was trying to dig her way up from the floor.

The glazed look in her eyes told me it was a concussion when I rolled her over, but her lips were moving weakly, trying to speak.

"Chess . . . Chess . . ." she mumbled.

"How'd this happen?" I whispered. "Who did this to you?"

She strained against me. "Where's Chess? What . . ."

"Don't worry about anything. Just tell me what happened. Somebody meant business, and they didn't mind letting the world know about it."

She closed her eyes tightly. "We were waiting for you . . . Chess and I. Someone rang from the front. Chess went out to see who it was . . . It's the butler's day off. I heard them coming back, so I came into this room."

"Who was it? Who was it came back with him?"

"Didn't see who it was . . ." She shook her head painfully. "I called out and asked . . . asked Chess had you arrived. He said no . . . and took whoever it was to the front again. In a while, I heard the door open behind me, thought it was Chess. That's all I remember . . ."

I looked over at Horvat's body crumpled on the floor. Whoever had bumped him had hung around long enough to take a couple of shots at me; they evidently knew I was on the way.

My guess was that the rub-out guy had a lot of his plans goofed this evening. Horvat even threw him for a loss. Both guys knew each other well enough for one of them to toss something into the other's drink. That might have been the reason for the return back up front. Meg Inglander would really have complicated things if she hadn't called out to Horvat.

This had been real luck for the guy. After he fed Horvat the fatal double dosage, all he had to do was come back and bust Meg Inglander in the head.

Up to that point, everything must have gone like clockwork for the guy. He probably had a good spot facing the door, just waiting for me to step through. But, right at the last moment, who should show back on the scene but Horvat! I bet the rub-out guy was so surprised he couldn't get himself together right away. Horvat held his own for a while, but the effects of the poison apparently got him.

The sudden rumble undoubtedly threw the other guy off his bearings. By the time I got there, he was too scrambled to carry off the ambush.

I looked down at Meg Inglander. She had lapsed into a semi-consciousness. A dark half-moon had just risen around the top and back of her head. Her full, curving body was heaped upon itself, the big breasts pointing upward helplessly. There was something about her body, the legs exposed up to the thigh, that made me draw up inside. For a moment, I actually couldn't move, feeling warm and cold together. I was able to turn away before the sweat came, but my heart was double stepping and it was all I could hear.

Somewhere under the shambles I found a phone and gave the operator a ring.

"Send a doctor over right away—emergency!" I left the receiver hanging down and went back to take another look at the girl.

I stopped before I got halfway, crying inside myself, like a baby or something. That feeling was riding me hard again, piggybacked, with a pair of cold fingers in my eyes.

Then the voice started talking, speeded up, like Woody Woodpecker, and it was laughing at me because I didn't have what other folks had, because I was tainted, like a leper, with a curse on my head.

It was no use trying to get around the facts: something was wrong with me.

And whatever it was was scary as hell . . .

Eleven

NEXT MORNING, IT WAS THE rye bottle as a sleeping companion again. My mouth was husky, but I didn't have a hangover. I got right up and ordered breakfast. On the way back, I stopped in the bedroom and put five spares in the .32's clip and gave the firing mechanism a good going over.

Guns. I knew them better than anything, from World War II, and those 90-day wonders and the mud. Like we were no better than mud. All of them could go to hell, that's what I told them. But I knew my guns, and they knew I knew. I knew heaters better than people, better than myself . . .

I'd gotten into a fresh suit when the phone rang.

"Yeah?"

"Mr. Sorrell?" It was Eversen.

"What happened to you last night?"

"I was trying to get a line on Lilly," he said from far away, like he was speaking under his hand. "After you called last night, I went out to the beach house to have a look around."

"What'd you find?"

"Nothing of interest, but Lilly surprised me before I could leave."

"What happened?"

"He wasn't in much of a mood to talk. He and Naida were together. I told them I'd come over to pick up a case of bonded. Lilly looked like he'd been in a fight somewhere."

"About what time was this?"

"Oh, between 10:30 or 11:00."

"That would be about right."

"What?"

"Is Lilly at the club today?"

"Not now, but he'll be around later on this evening."

"Good. Don't call me, I'll call you."

I put the receiver down. Everything was just gorgeous. Lilly was definitely in the pan. Luck had seen fit to make him blunder just once too often. All I needed now was about fifteen minutes alone with him and I'd know where that dough was.

IT WAS 1:35 P.M. WHEN I came out of the Hollitop. I hadn't even gotten around to the parking lot before Hendricks sidled up next to me and poked something in my ribs. Whatever the thing was was as round as an all-day sucker, but my luck these days always ran against the odds.

"Markle wants to see you downtown," he said happily. "I won't have to insist on you accompanying me, will I?"

"Not one bit."

"C'mon, I'm parked around front."

It's a funny thing about Hollisworth—nobody in that town notices a goddamn thing. Or at least they act like they don't notice a thing. A man and woman paused together at the front doors to watch Hendricks hustle me into the big Buick between the driver and himself, and they couldn't help seeing the gun. I'll lay odds they were tourists; nobody else gaped that way.

The uniformed driver had us downtown in a trice. Hendricks didn't talk and I was in no mood to carry on a conversation. I had an idea what it was all about, and Hendricks wasted no time relieving me of the .32 after we got to headquarters.

The building was an ugly brownstone. The hallways were dusty and looked unused, but with the syndicate setup in Hollisworth such a place is better unused. Even the pasty-faced cops looked unused.

We came to a stop on the second floor, where Hendricks gave a polite tap under the gold V in Markle's name on the door facing.

"Who's there?" the boss called out testily, as though we'd interrupted him in the bath.

"It's me," Hendricks said. "I've got our friend with us."

After a pause, Markle said, "Wait a minute." Then he opened the door.

When you see police captain Vin Markle in his office, you have seen everything. His official garb is a smoking jacket, red silk, and his staff of justice is a good shot of bourbon.

His office is anything but, excluding the bedroom blue desk, which modestly matched those fat sofas and chairs. He was a reader, that guy, and the place looked more like a den than anything else. The lingering scent of perfume and the half-open door leading off to another room told me the place had other uses, too.

"Sit down, Sorrell," he said, as though my name had a bad taste.

"Thanks."

Hendricks went over and posted himself by the door.

Markle perched on an arm of one of the chairs and took a swallow of the drink before going on.

"I see you're surprised at my choice of furnishings," he said finally.

"I'm in the wrong business."

"Which conveniently brings us to the point. You don't mind my getting right at it, do you?"

"Not at all."

"It's very simple, Sorrell. You're getting to be a pain in the ass."

"I could think of better spots."

"Fortunately, such is not your prerogative." He got up to close the door to the other room. "I can appreciate your ignorance of the way things go around Hollisworth. You were sent here to do a job and you've really done the best you could."

"You can't kick a guy for trying."

"The same doesn't very well apply for a fellow who louses things up."

"C'mon and pull me out of the heather, mother, you're not making any sense."

Hendricks smacked his palm with a fist. "Boy, this guy is a real comedian."

"That's just fine," Markle said. "He'll appreciate the humor in my telling him he's got just two hours to get the hell out of Hollisworth."

I didn't appreciate it. "Are you serious? It seems to me you're forgetting something."

"If you mean the boys on the council back in the big city, I'm glad to tell you this was their idea."

"You don't mind if I double check, of course?"

"If you think it'll do any good. I don't think you'll have time for that, though." He went over to the liquor cabinet and poured himself another drink. "You see, Sorrell, it's not your fault that you're stupid. I guess you were just born that way. Before you came, we knew Cassiday, Horvat and Benedict were slated to be eliminated and were told not to interfere. The job you did on Benedict was sloppy but adequate. Your low point was Chess Horvat."

"What are you talking about?"

"Last night, at the Inglander place. You made three very bad mistakes. You knocked the guy off beyond our jurisdiction, beat up one of the richest women in the state and were foolish enough to stick around long enough for her to plate you with an ID."

"It may not do any good to say this," I told him, "but Horvat was on his way out when I got up there. The guy who did it hung around to take a few shots at me. I found the Inglander dame with her head caved in while I was looking the joint over."

"You're right," Hendricks laughed, "it won't do any good!"

"Why don't you shut your fat mouth?" I snapped. "Maybe if I'd let you come along for the ride, you could verify the whole thing."

Markle regarded his flunky thoughtfully for a moment. "He's right, Hendricks. If you'd been on your toes, you probably could have caught Sorrell in the act, if you know what I mean. Think of the heat we'd have saved." He turned back to me. "I can't say I regret the whole thing, however, since we're off the hook either way around. Mr. Sorrell's penchant for assaulting young ladies has worked out just fine for us."

"Yeah, everything's just dandy for you," I said, standing. "But I'm not going anywhere until I'm told directly."

Markle picked up a slip of paper from his desk. "Perhaps you'd like to see the telegram I got from Lou Pulco this morning."

"I wouldn't believe it, anyway. Now if you'll just tell your lap dog to give me my heat, I'll get the hell out of here."

Markle gave me a wide, satisfied grin. "I'm sorry, Sorrell, but we're confiscating your weapon—for your own protection. You see, if you're not out of town at the specified hour you're going to be shot on sight."

"Sure, I understand. You're gonna make it as easy as possible."

"Precisely." He motioned for Hendricks to open the door. "Oh, yes, that spare you had in your rooms at the Hollitop isn't there anymore, a couple of my men saw to that last night."

"I expected as much."

He raised his glass in farewell. "Bon voyage, Sorrell. It has been so nice knowing you." He looked at his watch. "Remember, if you're still in town after three o'clock, we're going to kill you."

Twelve

I WAS ONE STEP AHEAD OF those guys.

I had an idea they weren't going to stick with the two-hour deadline.

After I'd gotten into a taxi out front, I had good reason to believe my doubts were at least half-right. Hendricks and a blue coat got into the Buick and came after me, and they didn't care if I knew it, either.

The cabby shot me right over to the Hollitop, with a fin for encouragement. I got out and went directly to my rooms. I tried to get Pulco at his office in New York, but his secretary told me he wouldn't be in for the rest of the day.

Lou'd given me an emergency address and phone number, but he told me never to call unless it was absolutely necessary. It couldn't get anymore necessary than it was right now, but I didn't get an answer when I rang the number up.

I called Western Union and had them send out a wire asking Lou to get in touch with me as soon as possible by phone, then I slammed the phone down and stalked helplessly around the apartment.

Boy, was I the prize patsy!

As of the past few days, I seemed to be born for putting my foot in it. The frame was a bit awkward but so was my head. I went into the bedroom and started throwing some of my things into a suitcase. If things were the way I expected, I'd really have to be traveling light.

In the back of my head, that little voice started whispering again, but I was already scared. If Lilly was my man, he couldn't have set the thing up better than if he'd planned it. But why would he do that, with my part of the job less than half-done?

It occurred to me then that I didn't know where the hell Cassiday was—for all I knew, he could be dead. The loose ends in this puzzle just didn't fit anywhere!

Where was the dough?

Where was Harv Cassiday?

And why was Chess Horvat dead?

The dough wasn't so hard. Lilly probably had it. I could even figure Horvat in on this. He was pressuring Lilly for his share, Lilly wouldn't come through, Horvat threatened to make a deal with me, Lilly killed him. Okay. Where was Cassiday? He had to be around somewhere, dead or alive. Maybe that's why Horvat had to be removed. Lilly had gotten rid of Cassiday and Horvat figured himself next.

It all sounded nice, but from where I sat—in the middle—it just wasn't convincing enough.

I finished packing and had the desk clerk send a bellboy up for my bag. I sat around for forty-five minutes, knocking off a quarter fifth of rye, then when I thought Hendricks and his buddy were just about ready to come up and see what the hell was going on, I slipped out of the apartment and went down to the service exit.

I was hoping Hendricks would take the precautions I thought he would, and he had. Down past the basement landing I could hear some guy with asthma breathing heavily. The guy was standing in the shadows, and from the outline he cast through the teeth of steps I could tell he wasn't expecting anyone to come through.

"Hey, mister," I called, exposing myself only partially at the head of the stairs.

"Huh, who is it?"

"The bellboy. Mr. Hendricks says for you to come around to the front."

"Oh . . ." I heard him stumbling up the steps.

I braced myself. When he puffed to the top I hauled back and rammed my fist into his soft gut, feeling his hot breath woosh out over my right shoulder. His gun was unholstered, and as he started falling down the stairs the thing went off twice.

He finally settled in a groaning heap at the bottom and I came all the way down. The poor sucker was damn near dead.

I took the long nosed .38 and a couple of slugs from his belt and vaulted across the basement to the express entrance. Luck smiled on me. The doors opened out on the parking lot, where the Impala stood waiting only about a hundred feet away.

I dashed over, got under the wheel and took off, with several important stops to make before I left town.

I was on my way—or so I thought. Two blocks away from the Hilltop I none too gently smacked into the side of a cruising cruiser.

I have a talent for such things . . .

"YOU," SAID VIN MARKLE, "ARE a damn fool, Sorrell."

I grinned appropriately. "What can I say after I say I'm sorry?"

I was back in Markle's boudoir-office, this time with my hands cuffed behind my back. Hendricks, along with four menacing blue coats, including the cop I'd walloped, hovered over me hungrily.

Markle, attired now in a gray business suit, leisurely observed me from behind his desk. "I've just made a call to the state police, you know. They'll be here momentarily . . . Oh, don't look so relieved, Sorrell. You're going to make an escape bid before they arrive."

"That's gonna make you look silly, isn't it?"

"Not as silly as it'll make you look, I'm afraid." He turned to Hendricks. "Have you got everything set up?"

"We're just waiting on your signal," Hendricks said, eyeing me with complete ecstasy. "We'll take him downstairs, he slugs me——"

"You didn't know I was double-jointed," I cut in.

"——he breaks through the side door, we blast him as he runs for the street."

"Perfect," Markle said, then to me: "Don't feel at all bad about it, Sorrell—we were going to kill you, anyway."

"I was afraid you didn't care."

Hendricks came over and gave me a bust in the nose. My head exploded with the pain.

"You should have been a comedian," he said.

Through the pain, I grasped for straws. These guys weren't kidding, and unless I was able to come up with a stall I'd never be in a position to return the fine favors they'd given me.

"Listen, Markle," I said, "you wipe me and you'll be wiping the chance of a lifetime."

He looked at his watch casually. "About ten more minutes, boys."

"The money, Markle—the half million Cassiday and his boys lifted! I know where it is!"

I struck a tender spot. Markle's eyes narrowed and he didn't say anything for a long time, then he got up and came over to sit across from me on the couch.

"You're joking, aren't you, Sorrell?"

"Oh, sure! I'm in a fine position to joke at the moment."

"If you know where the money is, why hadn't you got it and left Hollisworth before now?"

"Why do you think I was hanging around?" I said. "I had to be sure I was right."

The promise of death makes all voices sound sincere. Markle looked up at the blue coats and Hendricks. "Leave us alone for a moment."

The blue coats filed out, but Hendricks hung around.

"I said alone," Markle said.

"But, Vin——"

"Do as I say, you fool! You're not going to be left out on anything."

Hendricks followed the others out reluctantly, but I could see he wasn't at all convinced.

"All right, Sorrell, let's have it."

"What do I get out of this?" I said.

He smiled. "Why, your freedom, naturally. Suppose we let your escape attempt be a successful one?"

"What about my share of the dough?"

He shook his head sadly and clicked his tongue at me. "Please don't be a hog about this, Sorrell."

"What's going to keep me from going back and telling the boys in the big city that you've got the cash—that you had the cash all along?"

This point was very effective. "There's not much choice, is there, my friend? All right, we split——"

"Fifty-fifty," I said.

"Let's hear what you've got to say."

"All right," I said. "I've got it first hand that Brace Lilly was head man in the operation. He conspired with the three dodos to lift the plans and take off the bank caper. Benedict told me before I gave him the rub that he and the others were supposed to get the payoff here in Hollisworth a couple of months ago. Something went wrong, Lilly stalled them. It's my idea that Lilly never intended to split with them."

Markle began to laugh. "You expect me to believe that pansy was the brains in a half million dollar caper! Come, come, Sorrell, you'll have to do better than that!"

"It all figures. When I came on the scene, it made things perfect for Lilly. He sent his wife Naida over to my apartment to give me a lead on Chess Horvat. When I pressed, Horvat wanted to cop out. Meg Inglander came to see me and we arranged a meeting with Horvat. That's when I was fitted with the frame." I stopped for a second. "Does it make sense to you that Horvat would let me get close enough to him to feed him some poison?"

I could see the interest peeking out of Markle's dark eyes. "You say Lilly did it . . ."

"Who else? Remember how the joint was torn up when you guys got there, as though a fight had gone on? Lilly got back to his home later on that evening with his face chewed up."

Markle was rolling those things over in his head. "Interesting, Sorrell, but how can you boil all these things down to Brace Lilly?"

It was the same question I'd been asking myself all along, and

I still didn't have a reasonable answer. All my evidence against Lilly was circumstantial.

"It makes sense to me," I bluffed. "Lilly was central enough in the syndicate's operation and too obvious an individual to take such a chance. It wouldn't have been difficult to con those three saps in on the deal. When everything went against the plans I'd received in New York, Lilly tried to hustle things up and get me out of the way. I've an idea that Cassiday's already dead."

Markle watched me thoughtfully. "You portray Lilly as quite an ulterior force, Sorrell.

"Give me a few hours alone with him tonight," I said. "I'll get the money."

Markle didn't take as long trying to make up his mind as he would have had me believe.

"The money," he said. "You say you know where it is?"

"Lilly's got it. Let me go for a few hours and I'll get it for us." I was sure to add the plural.

He looked at his watch again. "You may have something, Sorrell. I'm taking a chance. We're going to let you escape—with provisions, of course. You won't be able to get out of Hollisworth, and if it becomes necessary for us to eliminate you, we will."

He went to the door and called in the blue coats and Hendricks.

"We're going on with the plans," he told them, "with a few variations." Then he outlined it to them, explaining that all slugs fired at me should be aimed a little bit high.

"But, Vin," Hendricks said discouragedly, "suppose it's just a trick?"

Markle winked an eye. "I don't think it would do Mr. Sorrell much good, do you?"

The coppers took me downstairs, where Hendricks snapped the cuffs off and I was able to get the blood circulating in my wrists again.

"There's the side door," he said disgustedly. "Take out past the garage and around the side drive. A plain black city car is parked at the curb with the keys in it, a Ford."

I patted him on the head and looked into the glowering face of the copper I'd clobbered earlier. "I hope your aim's good, fellas."

So I took off, and those guys really turned it on for the benefit of their fellow officers and anyone who might have been watching.

They were supposed to keep their shots up high, but I heard a bullet whistle past my ear by inches. A couple of them chopped and skidded across the pavement just in front of me, singing like maddened crickets.

But I made it, that was the important thing. It was strange, but the thought of dying didn't bother me so much. I just kept thinking that I wouldn't find that dough or be able to get Hendricks and Vin Markle, if I was clumsy enough to get killed.

I made it around to the side drive, where the black Ford was parked exactly as Hendricks said it would be. I got in and twisted the key starter, rammed the stick shift home to first and squealed out into traffic, scaring the hell out of two women wheelers and a truck driver.

Markle's sudden and urgent interest in the half million might have been surprising but for one thing, and I was slowly getting it together in my mind.

I know he didn't intend to split the money with me, if he found it, any more than I intended to come running to him, if I did. I began to smell another influence, and I mean literally.

I remembered the perfume odor when I came into Markle's office earlier that afternoon, and it was only now that my mind and nose made the association.

I'd smelled that perfume before—on Naida Torneau.

I was speeding down the city streets, but it didn't make too goddamn much difference now . . .

Thirteen

I HID OUT ON THE backroads till darkness gobbled up everything that evening, like a fat, black glutton.

My mind was going funny again, and I was getting real mad at nothing. My patsy personality was rebelling and I knew it was more than a mere warning.

Naida Torneau had been by to see Markle, assuredly. If her old man had the dough, why was she taking chances? When you're latched onto five hundred grand, it doesn't make much difference whether your true love is a sissy or a fish.

No, it had to be something else.

I found a roadside phone booth and gave the Hollitop a ring.

"Hello, Hollitop Terraces," the desk clerk said.

"This is Andy Sorrell. Have there been any calls for me today?"

I could hear him choke back the surprise. "Mr. Sorrell? Oh, Mr. Sorrell! Why, now, no, Mr. Sorrell, I haven't received anything for you in the past few hours I've been on."

"Anybody been looking for me?"

"What? Oh, no, no, Mr. Sorrell, no one's called!"

"What's the matter? You think this is an audition or some thing?"

"Oh, no, no, no, Mr. Sorrell! It's . . . I—well, could you possibly tell me where you are at the moment, Mr. Sorrell?"

I laughed at him. "No, I couldn't possibly. How many cops are there standing around the lobby now?"

"What . . . ?"

"You heard me, Hester. You tell me, or I'm gonna come right over and twist your goddamn lying neck off right down to the quick!"

His voice broke. "Please, Mr. Sorrell, I don't want any trouble! The state police have been in asking for you. They left three men here. I don't know anything about what's going on, please believe me!"

I hung up. Vin Markle didn't waste any time getting the weight off his neck. I looked at my watch and saw it tick out twenty past eight. Biting down on a hunch, I called up Lilly's and asked for Eversen.

"Mr. Eversen speaking," the guy said diplomatically.

"Sorrell, honey. Was just thinking of you and wondering if I should come over and blow a hole in your head for giving me a bum steer."

"But ... but I don't understand, Sorrell!"

"You know what I'm talking about. You said Lilly had the money. I don't think Lilly has the money."

"But it's the truth!" he said frantically. "From all I can gather, Lilly does have the money! What about Cassiday and Horvat and Benedict? And what about last night—when you were shot at? Lilly came in late, didn't he? It could have been him who attacked you and killed Horvat, couldn't it?"

"You ask too many questions, baby."

"But I'm right, Sorrell, you know I'm right!"

"Is Lilly around the club now?"

"No. He's supposed to have some of his friends in from Santa Monica later on tonight. He won't be in here at all."

"That makes it solid, friend. Since Lilly's going to have a leisure hour, I think I'll just stop in before it starts."

"Sorrell—"

I hung up before he started whining again.

I had to be on my tippy-toes, now that the state boys were after me. No doubt they'd have road blocks set up on the main highways and a couple of stakeouts at the busier joints, if they were convinced I hadn't left town yet.

I took the backroads, running into several dead ends, but it didn't take me over an hour to get within the vicinity of Lilly's beach house.

Remembering his playmates with the over-developed shoulders, I felt a bit naked. I left the car about three-quarters of a mile down the road and made myself a part of the crags and jagged upshoots on the beach.

The salt chopped into my nostrils and the wash of the sea and spray made my blood race, like I'd taken a good shot of rye.

The lights in Lilly's joint were just as gay as he was. The house, an eccentric construction, sat right on the edge of the water, with a tidewater mark. The basement was above water, and you could have dived in from the second floor balcony when the moon was high.

I galloped over to the side of the building and caught the rungs of a wrought-iron water lily lattice, formulating the obvious pun in my mind a little late. The thing took me easily to the second floor, where I was able to reach over and get a grip on the balcony. I hauled myself over and pressed my back against the wall.

Through a pair of single-paned doors I could look in on the colorful softness of a living room, and squaring off in the center like two gamecocks were Naida Torneau and Tina Meadows. It looked like what they were saying was real interesting, so I reached over and twisted open the door on my side until it was cracked about ten inches.

"I'm going to tell every goddamn thing I know!" Tina Meadows was saying. "You said I'd get Al's share after Sorrell killed him, but all I got was the run-around. I'm going to tell Vin everything!"

"You fool!" Naida snapped at her. "Don't you realize how high the stakes are now? If you say one thing, we'll both be killed!"

"What about the money? You told me if I buttered Al up enough, he'd tell me. He never told me one thing. All I got was two black eyes and a fractured shoulder where that bruiser worked me over."

Naida grabbed her by the arm. "Sorrell is out of the way now, stupid! I didn't find out till today how he'd been used. Now keep your mouth shut! By tomorrow night, we'll both be on easy street."

Tina snatched away from her. "We'd better, I'm just telling you— we'd better!"

She stalked out, with Naida close behind. I slipped into the room and over to the door. I opened it until I could look out.

Tina had just reached the landing from the circular staircase. She was still talking heatedly, but I couldn't make out what she said. Naida went over to the door with her and slammed it with relief after the visitor had made her jet-propelled exit.

She stood rubbing a hand thoughtfully across the bridge of her nose, then raised her head to call out to the closed doors of one of the lower floor rooms, "Lil, I'm going out for a while. Be back in time for the party."

There was a muffled response, and she went back to the rear of the house. In a moment, she returned with a braided shawl about her shoulders and went quickly out the front door.

I tipped down the stairs noiselessly and was able to watch her screech out of the attached garage in a black Thunderbird. The quartet of red eyes on its tail disappeared out on the road in a few seconds.

I swung my attention to that door Naida'd been talking to.

Something told me not to, but I decided to go for broke.

The first thing I saw when I entered was Brace Lilly, sitting in the midst of what must have been his private sanctuary. The walls of the room were lined with nudes—all men.

The next thing I saw was red flashes, and everything in front of me became a concave-convex illusion.

I knew I'd hit the jackpot again . . .

Fourteen

WHOEVER IT WAS MISSED OUT on his Sunday punch.

Whatever he hit me with chopped away a lot of flesh behind my right ear, but it did little more than knock me down and daze me for a moment.

I reached for him going down and was almost deafened by an explosion. He'd fired right in front of my eyes. The powder flash peppered my forehead, but I was able to swing my arm around, half-blinded now, and get a grip on his gun arm.

I dug my fingers in and wrenched. I heard the guy gasp and pull back, yanking me off balance, but he was playing hell trying to get away.

Desperation made him think of his knee as a weapon, and he gave it to me, but hard. I heard my teeth clack against each other in the back of my head. The blow was effective. I loosed my grip and heard the patter-patter of little feet as my guy got the hell out of there.

Way over around South Bend, the sound of a car gobble degooked around in my brain, as my head and the floor matched grains.

For a long time, I didn't know what the hell I was doing there. I was knocked out somewhere, on my hands and knees, feeling like a little kid who'd had a chance to wash out that bastard neighborhood bully and goofed it.

Finally, I was able to bring myself around. The little voice was talking again, frightening me, and I was so full of frustration it felt like I'd exploded.

My mouth was bleeding on the inside. The blood was good-tasting, warm and full of sea salt. Every goddamn thing in the world was against me, just like it'd always been all my frigging life.

When I could see again, I stood up. I had that feeling, and after looking into Lilly's ivory-pallored face I knew he was dead. I got that smell of Jergens lotion again.

It was a quick death, the kind which left the eyes open and a quasi-life expression on the mouth.

He was dressed for the party in a silky green, Mother Hubbard sort of thing with an open collar. He sat in a deep chair, with his arms at rest in his lap. An empty cocktail glass lay overturned on the floor.

I went over to him. I was so goddamn mad, I kicked him. "You sonofabitch," I said.

I punched him in his smooth face, making the head jerk, but I couldn't take that expression off. I punched him till my fist hurt, till that dead bastard hurt me.

Then I realized what I was doing, like in a dream where I'd been watching on, full of urgency in the need to have this dead thing living so that his bruised skin and my own would be gratified.

I was in a mental whirlpool. Where to go from here? What to do? That Lilly had died of poison was evident, and it was also indicated that his murderer was the same guy who'd conned Horvat out of his life.

But why?

I couldn't see the sense in the whole thing. Why was it necessary that Lilly had to be killed?

The only obvious answer was that he knew more than he should have known. The idea that he had the money was shot to hell now.

The complete recognition of where I was and under what circumstances came to me suddenly. I backed away from the body and went toward the door.

At the same moment, I heard a car drive up. I burst through the doors and stumbled up the stairs. I was lucky enough to make the top and fall into the room I'd come out of.

I cracked the door about a quarter inch and kept an eye on the ground floor. The doorbell chimed out. Then a pause. I heard a key in the lock and a quick snap as the door came open.

It was the little guy Eversen. He hesitated for a moment after entering, then passed out of sight under the staircase. In a few minutes he was back with a couple of fifths of something under his arm.

I came out and ran down the steps, cutting him off at the door. "Sorrell!"

I grabbed him not too gently by the lapels. "You sure make a lotta goddamn trips for that bonded, Pops. Why don't you hook up a conveyor from here to the club?"

He fidgeted around nervously in my hands. "It's Cutty Sark. We're all out at the club. Lilly doesn't keep any there—somebody's been stealing it," he said.

"Why'd you ring the bell?" I said. "You had a key—why didn't you just come right in?"

He tried to shrug away from me. "I don't know, Sorrell! It's—it's just something I do, that's all. I've been doing it all along."

"When was the last time you saw Lilly?"

"Earlier this afternoon, maybe this morning. That's when he told me about the party tonight."

I grabbed him by the neck and shoved him ahead of me into the room where I'd left Lilly.

He didn't react fast. When he saw that Lilly didn't move, he asked me if he were asleep.

"Go over and wake him up," I said.

He started over but turned before he got halfway. "Sorrell . . . Sorrell . . . what's the matter with him? Is he sick?"

"In the worst way."

"He's dead?"

"You catch on fast."

Eversen gave me a great big horror face and broke for the door, dropping both bottles of liquor. I caught him before he made it, hoisted him up on my forearms and slammed him against the wall.

"Don't! Please, don't, Sorrell, don't kill me, too! I won't tell!"

"Yeah, I'm made to order, right?"

He blubbered all over my sleeves. "Just let me go! Please, let me go! I don't want to have anything to do with this!"

"That's not gonna work out, my little friend," I said, applying a little pressure up where his collar plunged. "You put the finger on Lilly. You told me he was the one with the cash. You told me he was the one who'd engineered the heist. Now who else did you tell?"

"Nobody!" he choked out. "Nobody, Sorrell! Nobody but you!"

"Then that doesn't look so good for you, Pops. If I'm picked up by the police, I'm going to tell them it was you helped me knock Lilly off—and Horvat. I'm not gonna fry-ass by myself, you can bet on that!"

"Wait, wait, Sorrell, listen to me! Harv Cassiday slipped in the back way of the club this evening and pulled me off the floor. He said he was fed up with Lilly short-changing him and trying to have him killed—"

"Cassiday?"

"He's been up in Palo Alto. He said he got a telegram from Lilly this morning telling him to meet up this afternoon at the club for the split."

"Did he see Lilly?"

"No. Lilly'd been in for a few minutes and left. Cassiday said he was tired of the run-around and was going to settle things once and for all."

I eased up on the little guy's collar. "What you say would make sense except for one thing—you want me to believe Cassiday knocked off Horvat?"

"But why not, Sorrell? Wouldn't that make the split more promising? Benedict was already dead. With Horvat out of the way, Lilly and Cassiday would only have to split two ways. Now with Lilly out of the way—"

"Just hold on a minute, little fella," I said. "Where's the dough? The guy who knocked Lilly off didn't have time to leave with anything, I can swear to that."

"How do I know? Maybe Lilly stashed it. Maybe Cassiday found the hiding place, forced Lilly into telling him before he killed him."

In my mind I started thinking. That might be it, but I heard something in the distance that made the hair crawl up at the back of my neck.

"Police sirens!" I grabbed Eversen again and shoved him out in the hall. "I've gotta have somewhere to stay–quick! Where's your car?"

"Outside. The blue Pontiac. Here're the keys. I've got a cottage on this same road, about fifteen miles. You'll find the keys to it on the ring."

"Okay, but before you try anything funny I want you to give it a lot of thought. When the police get here, tell them you just arrived and found Lilly. Understand?"

Eversen looked scared to death. "I won't say anything wrong, believe me!"

I could see the headlights about a mile and a half down the highway when I came out front. I sprinted over to Eversen's late model Pontiac and got the thing started right up, keeping the headlights off until I'd gotten to the highway.

Then I turned all the horses loose, mashing down on the accelerator until the road behind me was nothing more than a hazy, gray-black blur.

Fifteen

I FOUND EVERSEN'S PLACE EASILY enough.

It was on the shaded side of a string of wind-blown trees, next to the sea. Perfect. The place was damn near impossible to find in the dark, so I knew it'd be hell to locate in the daytime.

The interior was modest but tastily equipped, with two bedrooms. A canted four panes allowed you to look out on the sea and the highway, simply by turning your head.

A ripple of distant bells came to me, and, looking at my watch with both its hands clasped together over the twelve, I realized with a shock that it was Sunday.

Sunday. All I could see about Sunday was a big wide church with a lot of bent heads and a guy in a white collar saying things he knew the people listening didn't give a damn about anyway.

Sunday.

I had been in Hollisworth nearly a week. It didn't take that long to put my life on the line. I'd come as the hunter, and now I was the hunted, that was for sure.

I fumbled around in the dark and found some cigarettes, lighted one. I let the coal sputter up and peter off with each draw, trying to think the way the guy who was putting me through these changes was thinking.

Three people were dead in less than a week, and I might as well have been responsible for all of them. Perhaps in a way I was.

Then being pulled off the job by Lou Pulco. Lou wouldn't have done that on his own, and I hadn't screwed things up so bad that I couldn't repair my missteps.

Granted, it did look bad for me, being on the scene when Horvat got his, and that Inglander broad put the clincher on. But she must have told them she'd seen me after she'd been slugged.

However, the syndicate's gripe was altogether legit—I had no business being seen at all. My job was to get in and out as fast as possible. Here I was, caught up in an assignment which shouldn't have taken over two days under normal circumstances.

But I was greedy, just like everybody else.

Naida Torneau was after that half million, and so was Tina Meadows, not counting Vin Markle, Harv Cassiday and the syndicate. My friend Eversen had some hidden motive, too, and it was not to play Tom Champion, boy hero.

I let my mind wander, like a magnet in a pin factory.

There was something I wasn't hitting! It was right there for me to see, but I kept putting my own thumbs in my eyes.

I'd get something out of this, or I'd be glad to die!

The conversation between Tina and Naida was provocative, and it certainly proved that my idea about me being a patsy was for real. Naida had an in. She knew a good deal more about the whole thing than anyone else, I was sure of it!

I heard the sirens again.

I crouched down and crawled over to the window. That bastard Eversen, I thought, but the car kept right on down the road in the direction of Lilly's.

I got up and stumbled around the place until I found some liquor in a recessed shelf of the kitchen sink. It wasn't rye, but I drink bourbon along with the rest.

I came out and sat down in the dark. My mind started picking those things up again, and I didn't try to stop it.

Where was the money? Cassiday wouldn't knock Lilly off unless he knew exactly where the money was, and Lilly wouldn't be fool enough to tell him unless he'd been unduly pressured. And from the looks of Lilly, he hadn't been forced to give up anything but his life.

Had Cassiday made a mistake? Maybe Lilly'd fooled him into thinking the money was somewhere it wasn't.

Who else could get close enough to Horvat and Lilly to feed them the poison? It had to be Cassiday, certainly. He'd been working with them. They trusted him.

But somehow, I just couldn't feature Cassiday poisoning anyone, that was the rub. Poison was more of a woman's weapon. And why not? Naida Torneau had seemed more than informed about what was going on.

She could have gone up to the Inglander place and fed Horvat the poison.

I bumped my head here. Naida needed more than a round shoulder to send Meg Inglander to dream land, and I knew for a fact that Naida had round shoulders.

By the same token, Lilly wouldn't have been such an easy victim. She'd even called to him before she left—and for whose benefit?

No, it hadn't been Naida. This brought me back around to Cassiday again. But where did that leave me? If Cassiday had the dough, he certainly wasn't wasting time in Hollisworth. In that case, I was left in the cold in my birthday suit.

I couldn't hide out forever, not with the state cops sniffing after me and Vin Markle prepared to sacrifice me at any moment.

For some reason, I had a hunch Cassiday was still around Hollisworth somewhere, which meant he didn't have the cash.

And another thing: Why didn't Cassiday kill me when he had the chance, if it was Cassiday who slugged me? He'd fired once with no effect, but after I'd wrestled with him and got that solid knee jolt it wouldn't have been difficult for him to play duck shoot while I drooled all over the floor.

I stopped thinking. The back of my head was burning now. I went back and found the liquor bottle again and brought it back with me into the living room. I stood for a long time watching the sea.

A squall was coming up close to shore and the first speckles of fine raindrops blew across the canted windows. The night was reasonably clear, though, and in the distance I could see a small white sail. I wondered to myself what goddamn fool was out on a night like this, then I had an idea . . .

Today was Sunday, the last day, and I was going to make it a good day for myself.

I remembered vaguely that Carolyn liked Sunday mornings, two shades of pink beneath the covers early Sunday morning, her breasts rising up under the softness of silk as she stretched her goddess body and breathed that smell of herself on me.

I began to tremble, looking out on the water.

I stood there and drank the whole goddamn bottle . . .

Sixteen

SOMEHOW I SLEPT.

What woke me was Eversen shaking the hell out of my arm the next morning. I sat up but the roof caved right in, like it always does when I drink bourbon.

"Get me something for this," I said, holding my head tilted so it wouldn't fall off.

The little guy scooted out and returned in a few minutes with a couple of Bromos and a glass of water. I didn't waste any time getting it down, and I was tempted to put my head in a stocking so none of the pieces would fall out.

"What time is it?" I croaked.

"Almost twelve," Eversen said. He was dressed for leisure in a gaudy sport shirt and slacks, and I could see now that the little guy wasn't as little as I'd first thought he was. The wide shoulders and thick forearms made his small hands seem almost deformed. Seeing him like that, the gray hair didn't make him look so old, either.

I struggled up. "You got anything to eat around here?"

He nodded quickly. "I thought you'd be wanting something. I've got some bacon and eggs going, and a grapefruit for that hangover."

"You can junk the grapefruit. Where's the bathroom?"

"The door behind you. Oh, yes, you'll find some things I picked up in town for you. I knew you didn't have anything to change into."

I got up and wobbled back to the bathroom, holding my head with both hands.

After I'd slipped down in the shower twice, I got out and found the "things" Eversen'd picked up in town for me. It was a beige Bermuda ensemble with white bucks and matching knee-length socks. Being a conservative dresser, I really considered this extreme, but under the circumstances the outfit might work out nicely.

I was feeling a little better after I'd got into them, but my stomach went deaf, dumb and blind when I sat down across from Eversen at the kitchen table.

"Just bring me a bowl and the coffee pot, Pops," I said miserably.

I heard Eversen laugh for the first time, like a little chipmunk. "I don't see anything so goddamn funny," I said.

"No, Sorrell, please forgive me," he chittered. "I was just thinking, here you are with practically the whole State of California looking for you—and you're nursing a hangover!"

He brought the coffee pot over from the stove and waited until I'd poured a cup and had my first sip.

"Vin Markle was over to the club last night," he said. "And this morning, all the employees had to return for questioning."

"That's not surprising," I said.

"Markle thinks you killed Lilly," he went on.

"That's not surprising, either. I was made for the role. And just where am I supposed to keep my stock of poison, in a hollow leg or something?"

"Poison?"

"Didn't Markle tell you? Lilly was poisoned, and so was Horvat. I've seen some poisons work; and this looks like one of the cyanides to me, probably prussic acid. There's a hell of a sweetish smell to the stuff, but the killer probably covered it up in a mixed drink."

Eversen looked confused. "I don't understand. It couldn't have been you, Sorrell."

"And why couldn't it?"

"Why—because you're not the type to use a poison. You'd use a gun or knife, wouldn't you? Or maybe your hands, like in Benedict's case."

"You'll make a fine character witness," I said. "Anyway, poison is the woman's choice."

"You mean Naida?"

"Possibly, or maybe Tina Meadows."

"I don't think it was Naida," he said thoughtfully.

"Truthfully, I don't either. Neither do I think it was Tina." I finished the cup and poured another, my brain beginning to oil up a bit. "When I got over to Lilly's last night, Naida and Tina were together. I don't think either one of them knew Lilly was dead. Naida left directly after Tina, and she called out to Lilly before she left. She wouldn't call out to anyone she already knew was dead, naturally. I think it was the murderer who answered her—the voice was muffled."

"Who could it have been?"

"I don't have much of a choice. I think Markle can safely be excluded. That leaves only three other people: Hendricks, Cassiday … and you."

Eversen's reaction was violent. "But you know I didn't have anything to do with it! What reason would I have for killing Lilly, just give me one!"

"I can give you five hundred thousand reasons."

"But I didn't know what was going on! I came in and got the liquor, you know that! The next minute you were dragging me into the room! How could I have killed Lilly? I'd just got there!"

"Relax, Pops," I said, smiling. "I can't fit you in anywhere as the killer, but I've got an idea you know more than you're telling. Why all the help? Whyn't you just call the cops and get me off your back?"

He was flustered, trying to find a reason. "Why—why, you made me, Sorrell! You're making me do this!"

"Yeah, I'm scaring the hell out of you."

"But, Sorrell—"

"You just keep right on doing what you're doing, Pops, and no mistake!" I said menacingly. "Maybe you'll get exactly what you're looking for out of this."

This pacified him a bit. "I think Cassiday did it, that's what I think." His eyes brightened suddenly. "Why couldn't it have been Lilly himself? He could have poisoned himself, couldn't he? And Horvat—he was even up at the Inglander place the night Horvat was poisoned, wasn't he?"

"There you go, asking those damn questions again. For one thing, Lilly didn't poison himself and then call the cops. Whoever called the cops thought I'd still be cooled there in the house, which would have wrapped things up perfectly. Unless I've taken a hell of a wrong road, I take Cassiday for the kind of guy who plays for keeps. He would have made sure the job was finished himself."

Eversen looked at his watch. "I'm going over to the club to supervise the cleanup work. Is there anything you want me to do?"

"Yeah, go over to the Hollitop and nose around. See if you can bribe one of the juniors to release my bags. Get the hell right out of there if you see any cops. Just act like you've got nose trouble. Give me a ring back here when you've taken care of that." I thought of the idea I'd had last night. "Is there any place around here where I can rent a boat, a small one?"

He scratched his head for a minute. "There's a public dock about five miles down the beach, but you'd probably be recognized there. I've got a skiff out in the garage. It may leak a bit, but it's seaworthy. What have you got in mind?"

"I think I'll take a little jaunt over the bounding main," I said. "I'll let you know how it turns out."

"Well, I'll be on my way," he said, getting up. "I'll ring you back at the first opportunity."

"I'll wait until you do."

After Eversen had left, I went over to the phone and dialed up New York again, the private number Lou had given me. I had trouble with the connection, but finally got it.

A woman answered and told me she was Pulco's private secretary.

"I'm Andy Sorrell. I'd like to talk with Mr. Pulco." ·

She didn't answer for a long time. "Mr. Pulco is not in at present," she said finally, "but he left a message in the event you should call, Mr. Sorrell."

"Let's have it."

"Mr. Pulco says you are to continue as directed until otherwise notified," she said in brisk, business-like tones. "Mr. Pulco would like to see you personally in his office by the middle of next week. Mr. Pulco says he would advise you to finish your assignment with all necessary speed."

"Does Mr. Pulco advise that I sprout wings and fly home?" I said caustically. "Or maybe I could sail through the Gulf and up the New England coastline."

"I beg your pardon, Mr. Sorrell?"

"Forget it. Just tell Mr. Pulco that I got the message."

I hung up. Mr. Pulco sure wasn't clearing this goddamn mess up any for me.

Markle said he'd gotten a telegram from Lou telling me to get home. He could have been lying, of course, but I didn't think so.

Why should Lou take me off the job, then put me right back on?

I could attribute this to my good buddy Markle without too much trouble, at least the part about me being taken off the assignment. Lou'd probably had a change of mind after thinking it over. Anyway, I still had Cassiday to go. I'd dealt with Pulco before, and this was the only time I'd ever goofed. Lou knew it; maybe that's why he was giving me a chance to clean up.

I went back to the kitchen, found another bottle and had a good shot of the dog's hair.

Lou's show of confidence made me feel a lot better. Now all I needed was a gun, and I'd be in business.

Seventeen

EVERSEN'S SPORTING SKIFF WASN'T IN the best of shape.

The stationary sprite had been broken off at the top and the leg-of-mutton sail looked like a piece of somebody's tattered underwear.

It was equipped with oars, though, and I flexed my muscles, remembering the days I could pull a fifteen-foot sharpie around the world, and then I was only a twelve-year-old kid.

Getting behind the dolly, I was able to wheel the thing out in the sunlight and check for leaks. I went into the house and got a bucket of water. I sloshed it over the bottom and got down on my hands and knees to take a look.

There were three leaks, one at the bow and two next to the centerboard.

I went back to the garage and was lucky enough to find a can of aluminum caulking. It had hardened some, but was still pliable enough to rake out with the end of a cold chisel.

I went back out to the boat and started giving it a good going over.

I pulled my shirt off under the sun. The sweat started popping out all over my body, and I began to feel goddamn good. It was like my boyhood, on the sea with my old man, him saying, "Watch your work, boy. You love her right, fix her right, and she'll never let you down. Take some sand and rub her nose . . ."

It was real good. I took the skiff off the dolly and turned her belly up. I got me some sand in the bucket and a piece of the canvas rigging, and I began to rub. I rubbed until her goddamn belly was slick and wood new, and all the time I was listening for my old man's approval, his nod.

All of a sudden, I was looking out to the sea, and my old man was dead, and I was wondering. Why, why, you sonofabitch up there, why'd you have to take my old man?

It was no good without paint. I didn't have the paint. My old man would never have allowed me to rub a boat without paint. My mother, my old man . . . and then Carolyn . . .

I began to feel funny. I wanted to crush something. I got down in the sand and grabbed two handfuls. I squeezed them until the sand was nothing in my hands, like all three of those people. I looked out on that big sonofabitch of a sea and I could hear things, voices, and they got louder and louder, and I stood up and hollered at them, like I'd hollered at that guy who came to get me after my old man had died.

"Don't catch me, you bastard!" I hollered, tears in my eyes. "I won't let you catch me! None of you can catch me!" And I ran and I ran and I ran.

Away . . .

I WAS ALMOST PLASTERED WHEN Eversen called that evening.

I'd forgotten where the phone was, but I finally found it under the sofa where it must have fallen. Luckily, the receiver hadn't come off. The room was a shambles. I'd been throwing things around, and I didn't have any shirt on.

Eversen sounded excited when I picked the phone up. "Sorrell, I was able to get in with the desk clerk. You got a telegram from some fellow named Lou Pulco this morning. He says for you to carry on your assignment, whatever that means. Markle picked the message up."

"Okay. Anything else?"

"Markle also confiscated your luggage. The police commissioner has arranged with the state people to handle your case strictly for Hollisworth. They're claiming you for the Benedict murder. A receptionist at Blue Haven gave your identification."

"I'm glad the state is off my ass," I said. "Now I'll only have to put up with Markle and his boys."

"That may not be so good. I hear Markle's out for blood."

"So am I. How're things over at the club?"

"Business as usual," he said. "Lilly's demise didn't affect Naida gravely. She says it'll be good for the trade."

"That's one way to look at it. Where is the bereaved widow?"

"Over at the beach house, celebrating, I think."

"Good."

"Are you going over?"

"I'm thinking about it. Don't call back if anything turns up. I most likely won't be here."

"All right. You can reach me at the club, if you need to call."

I rang off and sat with my head in my hands a long time.

I was trembling again.

It was so hard to figure out! Sometimes I would be all right, then zip! I'd go off my rocker again.

I went outside and found my shirt where I'd taken it off that afternoon. It was getting dark fast. It was 8:30 by my watch.

I wrestled the skiff back on the dolly and pulled it down to the edge of the water. It didn't take long to drag it out, and in a few minutes I was rowing through the gentle swells.

The sea was unusually calm, and although it was dark you could look around for miles. The sun had left a somber residue of illumination.

The oar hooks protested like squeaky old men under the rhythmic pull of my shoulders. It wasn't long before I saw Lilly's beach house in the distance. I took my shirt off again and dropped it in the bottom of the boat. If anyone spotted me, I wanted them to think I was some college kid out for a night of exercise.

It took me fifteen minutes to pull abreast of the place. I kept on down the shoreline, making sure nobody was hanging around. When I was about a mile away, I stopped and let the boat drift, like I was taking a breather.

I stayed like that for a half hour, waiting for the darkness to thicken, then I swung around and headed back.

I could see the lights burning from the same room I'd gone up to the night before, only this time the doors to the balcony were open.

I made good and damn sure I wasn't sticking my neck out before I came up on the beach. The exposed basement provided an excellent shelter from the front, so I pulled the skiff up on the beach as far as possible, catching hell a couple of times when the centerboard bogged down in the sand.

Since I had such luck the last time with the lily lattice, I tried it again. This time nobody was around when I got to the top.

As I came in, I could hear a hi-fi sounding off somewhere on the floor I was on. When I opened the door to the hallway, the music seemed to be jumping through the open doors of what looked like the master bedroom.

This time I wasn't taking any chances. A nude in ebony stood with her arms over her head under a lampshade near the door. I took the shade and light bulb out and snatched the cord out of the socket, wrapping it around the length of the figurine. The thing had a satisfying heft in my hand.

I came out and went down the hall. I exposed my head, but just enough for me to glance in with one eye. What I saw really jolted me.

Naida Tomeau was lounging on the couch in what must have been her private bedroom, eyes closed. She, unlike her husband Lilly, was very much alive, and she was dressed in nothing, from tip to toe.

I saw her mouth part, and the eyes opened and caught me before I could duck out of the way.

"Don't be bashful, Sorrell," she murmured, smiling at me. "Come on in . . ."

She covered herself ineffectually with a gown or something. I came in, closing the door behind me.

"Are you sure I won't be a bother?" I said, watching her swing her long legs around and prop herself up in a sitting position.

"I'm just in the mood to be bothered," she said seductively. "I seem to remember you didn't have a shirt on the last time we met. I think that black young thing fits you a lot more attractively than that muggy old pistol, though."

I came over to her, but my mind wasn't clicking anymore.

A long time ago I remember hearing some guy talk of an experiment which had to do with rats, in which a male and female were placed in respective cages. The male rat was starved for several days, then put into the cage with the female, where there was plenty of food.

"It's the damnedest thing!" this guy said. "That crazy rat'll go after the tail before he eats!"

What that test proved then, I don't know, but it sure let me see that rats and men have a lot in common. Here I was, about to have my ass scissored, staring down at something that had C'mon, sucker written all over it.

"I've been expecting you, Sorrell," she said, extending a hand to pull me down next to her.

"So I see."

"Don't be frightened," she cooed, like I was a little kid afraid of the bogey man. "No one's going to be back tonight. . . ." She leaned over and put her lips against mine, backed away when she didn't get any response.

"What's the matter, Sorrell?"

"Don't you feel a little funny screwing around with the guy who knocked off your old man?"

She pooh-poohed. "You know I don't believe that damn old crap! And even if I did, how will I ever repay you for the favor?"

"In hundred dollar bills."

"What?"

I wasn't getting through to her, so I pointed to the center of my palm and told her to take a good look. When she had her eyes fastened to the spot, I let her have it right on the kisser.

Her head snapped back with the force of the blow and she grabbed her mouth to see if any teeth were missing.

"You bastard!" she yelled. "You sonofabitching bastard!"

She made a hook of her fingers and tried to tear out my right eye, but I ducked and let her have it again, this time harder. She wasn't used to this kind of treatment, or at least she hadn't received a dose in a long time. I took her around the merry-go-round two more times, until I thought the cobwebs were closing in.

"Okay," I said. "Do we begin again, or do we act sensible about the whole thing?"

"You goddamn crapping bastard!" she hollered, raking my chest with her fingernails. "You dirty, crapping sonofabitchl'

I got away from her and cuffed both her ears. While she was trying to dig the bees out of her skull with her fingertips, I found the black statuette and pulled the stiff plastic cord off. The gown had fallen away and all those pink spots were like fuzzy peaches. I doubled the cord up and laid it briskly against her thigh.

"I'll kill you!" she cried, coming at me, but I stepped aside and snapped the cord against her rump twice. She tripped and fell. She landed on her side, and I was there to welcome her home.

I beat her ass until her whole body was crisscrossed with welts and her spasmodic jerking accompanied the thunder of the hi-fi. She was making small animal sounds on the floor, and she wasn't trying to get up.

I didn't know what was happening until she dug her fingernails into my leg and began kissing it!

"Darling!" she screamed joyfully. "My darling baby, my sweet! Please don't stop! Please don't ever stop!"

Her body, crisscrossed with livid welts, wiggled and shook on the floor. Her breasts pressed hot and firm against my knees. I felt myself rising as her hand came to my waist, clawed at my loins. Her buttocks, round, cherubic, seemed somehow profaned with the red stripes, twisted against the floor with wild passion.

It was like a nightmare. I was unable to stop her hands from doing things to me. I pulled away from her, and she sat back on her haunches, a hand under each breast, raising their pink mouths high and questing toward me.

"Oh, you bastard!" she screamed. "Take me—take me before I go crazy!"

Eighteen

THERE'S A LITTLE BIT OF the queer bug in all of us.

Naida's ecstasy was infectious. I got her up and dragged her over to the massive bed. She was wiggling in my hands like a boa, full of strength.

"Quick, Sorrell! Hurry, darling, hurry!"

I'd forgotten everything, but absently I was aware of a victory. As I knelt over Naida, watching her firm breasts and their nipples touched with the scarlet of passion, the flesh pulsating along her belly and thighs, I felt the utter conqueror.

I made myself ready, but hesitated purposely, wondering at the thing unleashed within her.

"Please, Sorrell! Please don't torture me!"

With a great sense of objectivity, I sunk myself into her hotness and fire . . .

I SAW HER COME OUT of a dream.

We were entangled on the bed, and she was breathing heavily under me, her lips shiny with a smear of blood from some small wound.

She began kissing my mouth, my throat. "Oh, I love you, Sorrell! Honey, I love you more than anything!"

I was suddenly repulsed. It wasn't like the first time I'd had her, before I knew. Now I saw the affinity between her and Lilly, and it was as though I'd become a part of it.

I'd never felt like I'd betrayed Carolyn before by having another woman, but now I felt it as keenly as the pains a woman feels in labor.

The taste of her was in my mouth. Her arms seemed to have me glued to her breasts. I snatched away from her and went into the bathroom attached to her room. I had to wash up, I had to get clean again for Carolyn.

When I came out she had the gown on. She was still on the bed, sitting up against its padded headboard, but she'd gotten up somewhere along the line and made a couple of drinks.

"Come on over here, darling," she purred.

"I don't need the big build-up again," I said, but I went over and got the drink, horsing it down.

"Don't be cruel, Sorrell," she said pitifully. "Be gentle with me, lover."

"The next time I'll just use my fists. I think you and I would both like that better."

She reached out and grabbed me about the waist, put her head against my stomach. "Sorrell, I can't help it if I'm that way. Don't condemn me!"

"I don't give a damn what way you are," I said, pushing her away. "I wanna know where that goddamn money is, and baby, I'm almost sure you know the hiding place!"

"But I don't! I swear to you I've no idea where it is."

"You listen," I said, sitting down next to her. "I was here last night. I heard you and Tina Meadows talking in the next room. You told Tina that tonight both of you would be in the chips, after she raised hell about what you'd promised her for being nice to Al Benedict."

"But I didn't promise her anything," she said. "Benedict himself promised it to her. Just before they stuck up the bank, Benedict used to come around to the club all the time to watch her dance. To get on her good side, he told her he had a big deal coming off and he'd treat her right. After he came back to Hollisworth and went into the sanitarium, he told Tina he'd see that I got the money for safe-keeping, that I'd be given her share."

"You didn't have any private deal with her, then?"

"Of course not, Sorrell! How could I?"

"Tina said you'd promised her a share if she found out where the dough was."

She knew now that I'd heard a good deal of what she and Tina had been talking about. "All right, darling, so there was a deal. But so what? Can you blame me for trying to get the lion's share?"

"No, but I can damn well blame you for trying to front me off. When you came to my apartment, you told me just the place to find Horvat. How did you know where he was?"

"From Tina, of course. She was seeing Benedict regularly. He told her practically everything, except where the money was."

"What are you and Vin Markle holding hands about, as if I didn't know?"

Her face blanched. "Markle . . . ? Why, I don't know what you mean. I know him, if that's what you're getting at."

"You know damn well that's not what I'm getting at," I said. "You wear a perfume that's a distinction in itself. I smelled it yesterday when the bulls strong-armed me up to Markle's office. You hadn't been gone more than a few minutes."

She looked away from me, gathering herself. "It shouldn't be hard for you to understand, Sorrell . . ."

"Shouldn't it?"

"Well, my goodness, no! Markle isn't an ugly man, you know. In fact, he's very handsome."

"Isn't that playing it a little too close to home? Markle made it plain when he gave me that going-over that it was because I'd jacked up Tina Meadows." I watched her face. "Don't tell me you didn't know. Tina even mentioned Markle last night by his given name. I don't think you're in the dark about the romance."

"What difference does it make?" she said, obviously piqued. "Who I want to go to bed with is my business!"

"Especially if your business concerns half a million dollars."

She swung off the bed and pranced over hotly to find a cigarette on the coffee table.

"You're not making any sense, Sorrell!" she said.

I began to laugh.

She pivoted around, and I could see I was getting under her skin.

"What's so goddamn amusing?" she said.

"The thought that I'm not the only patsy in this thing," I said. "I'd like to see Markle's face when he wakes up and finds himself wearing the blue ribbon!"

She came over to the bed, her manner changed quicker than a chameleon's colors. She sat down beside me and gave me the Lizabeth Scott routine. "Let's take and get the hell out of here, Sorrell. Markle doesn't mean anything to me—he never has. I can get the money for us; it'll just take a little time.

"From what I understand, it shouldn't take you over fifteen minutes. I hear Lilly arranged to lift that poke, along with the Three Stooges!"

"Who told you that? George Eversen?"

"How'd you know?"

"He's always sticking his nose in," she said. "The old bastard's got a crush on me. He's always hated Lilly. Don't believe anything he tells you."

"Lilly wasn't involved?"

"Lil never had a passion for anything but men—real men. I married him six years ago just to get away from Frisco. His old man left him some dough, and one of the provisions of his will was that his son got married in order to collect." She sighed disgustedly. "I guess the old guy thought that would make a man of him."

"Then where is the money?" I said. "If Lilly didn't have it, who did?"

"Why, the guys who stuck up the bank, naturally. They stashed the dough here in Hollisworth after the robbery, then split up. Benedict went to the sanitarium, Horvat up to his girlfriend's place and Cassiday out of town."

"Everything is falling into position too easy," I said. "Cassiday is the only one left. If he knows where the money is, why doesn't he just come in and pick it up and get the hell out of town?" She tapped my nose with a forefinger and winked. "All that would be fine, if things could work that smoothly. But the fact is, the money isn't where Cassiday thinks it is."

"I'm not gonna play games all night long," I told her. "Where is that goddamn money?"

"Be patient, Sorrell! Maybe you'd like to know where Cassiday is, instead."

"I wouldn't give a damn if Cassiday was hung up in that closet. I'm scheduled for the gas chamber, and if I go there's gonna be a hell of a price tag on the chair they strap me in."

"But don't you see?" she said, almost pleadingly. "We can't do anything with Cassiday hanging around. He knows I've got a lead on the money and he's going to keep me spotted until I pick it up. He's got to be put out of the way! You even got a telegram today telling you to finish him off."

"Did Markle read it to you?"

She smiled secretly. "How else would I know?"

I smiled back at her, but it was at the thought of how big a sucker she thought I was. "Okay. I knock off Cassiday. When do we get the dough?"

"I thought it'd be tonight, but I've run into some difficulties. It'll be tomorrow night. I'll be here waiting after you finish up."

"There's something I'd like to know," I said, getting up. "Who killed Lilly?"

She took on a modest mien. "Why, I did, baby. He was becoming too much of a bother."

I grinned down on her as though impressed. "Oh, yeah, one other little thing. Where is Cassiday now?"

"It's a rooming house on Deacon Street, an old folks' home. You won't have any trouble finding it."

"How'll I know him?"

"Why, hon, just ask for the youngest guy in the house! I think he's staying there under the name of Anderson."

"There'll be no slip-ups? No double-cross?" I said.

She got up and put herself against me, her arms around my neck. "Sorrell, you're the most upsetting thing I've ever met in my life! Just think of the things we can do together with that money." She pasted her lips on mine. "It wasn't all together true when I said I loved you—but I could . . . very easily."

"Don't let me down, Naida," I said with some authenticity. "I couldn't stand for everything to blow up right now."

"It won't, darling," she said, kissing me again. "Take my word for it—everything'll be just peaches."

I wanted to choke the tongue out of that lying bitch.

Nineteen

I DIDN'T SLEEP MUCH THAT night.

I sat up most of the time with one of my bottled Nemesis, trying to get everything synchronized.

That Naida was trying to make me the goat again, there was no doubt. I didn't believe she had the money, but I did believe her when she said she knew where to put her hands on it. I also began to understand her relationship with Vin Markle: she needed help to get that money. And she needed me as a foil.

I had to play my cards right, or things would turn out just as she had them planned. Her insistence on having Cassiday removed struck me as highly significant. Cassiday was hanging around, but it was my bet that he'd been told to.

I could fit Tina and Vin Markle into the scheme of things readily, but I still couldn't explain Horvat or Lilly.

Had Lilly poisoned Horvat, and then himself? For what reason?

I'd had things nicely figured out with Lilly clipped as the headman, but his sudden expiration really screwed up my former ideas. I was positive that Naida hadn't done it, or Tina Meadows. Anyway, that smell of Jergens on Horvat and Lilly told me both boys had been done in by the same person, and I couldn't see either one of the female principles in this act waltzing around that art gallery with Horvat.

I hadn't given up on Vin Markle or Harv Cassiday, and I hadn't failed to notice the interest of Markle's straw-haired sidekick when the subject of that half million came up.

But which one of the three?

I knew the question was going to be answered for me in some way—and soon.

I WOKE UP IN BED for a change the next morning.

I showered and shaved, expecting to smell the coffee perking in the kitchen, but when I got out there the stove was bare. I looked in Eversen's room, but he wasn't anywhere around.

I saw by the kitchen clock that it was after twelve. Eversen must have gone over to the club.

There was some bacon and eggs in the refrigerator and it wasn't long before I had a pair of skins and two sunnysides on a plate. It was the first food I'd had in a good while, and my stomach seemed surprised that I'd cared to think of it.

I was left with hunger pains after I'd finished, but I didn't feel like going through the motions again.

When I came back to my room again I saw that Eversen had dug up a suit and accessories for me somewhere. This beat the hell out of the Bermuda get-up, as far as I was concerned. However, I wouldn't need them till later, since it'd be plain suicide to get out during the daytime.

I lounged around for about an hour, trying to think out a workable method of operation. Then I got down to my jock strap after my food had settled some and went down to the sea.

It's been years since I swam against the sea's strength, let its big rough hands swamp me over with their many tons of water. I forgot all about myself. I swam until the sea and I were one and my waning power was fused in the great veins of that big bastard.

When I couldn't swing my arms any longer, I flopped over on my back and let the swells pillow me in their breasts and carry me slowly back to the shoreline.

I lost track of the time, swimming around out there. It was almost 4:00 p.m. when I got back to the house. Eversen still hadn't returned.

In the bathroom, I found a big terrycloth towel to dry off on. I went into the bedroom with the idea to put on those clothes, but I remembered Eversen had the car and I'd have to wait until he got back, so I slipped into the shorts and shirt again and found another bottle in the kitchen. All that was left was Scotch. It wasn't hard to figure out who'd been lifting Lilly's bonded.

I came back into the living room, and that's when I felt the guy. I didn't see him, you understand. It was just one of those things where you feel somebody staring at you.

He was on the kitchen side of the canted windows, and as I sat down on the couch I fumbled around with the bottle in order to get a good look at him from the side of my eye. I breathed a sigh of relief when I caught a glimpse of the sweatshirt.

I suddenly acted as though I'd forgotten something in the kitchen and went back quickly. Easing through the back door, I tipped around the side of the house, where my guy was still looking over the inside intently.

The soft-soled bucks and sand were made for each other. I came up behind him noiselessly until I was just a few feet away.

"Hey, Rube!" I yelled.

The guy almost jumped out of his britches. I blasted that look of shock off his face when he turned, a thumping left hook that smashed in just under the jawline.

The blow might have been effective if the guy hadn't been so scared. He stumbled back against the house and came at me with a right cross that could have been wicked, but I got out of the way. Then I gave it to him again as he came past, a short, smashing right to the kidney. He did a double take and crumpled in slow motion, a sucked-in expression on his face as he tried to draw wind back in.

He flopped squarely on his ass and stayed that way, both hands clasped to his side.

I had a good look at him while he was like that. He wasn't a little guy, but you couldn't call him big, either. He had that rusty red look the sun gives you, and the bell-bottomed jeans he wore gave me the real clue.

I reached down and pulled him up to my level. "All right, my friend, just what the hell are you doing around here?"

"I'm looking for a fella," he gasped shortly. "You didn't have to go and beat up on me like that, I wasn't doing anything."

"What ship are you on?"

"The S.S. Maribou. I've got a three weeks' leave. I'm down here vacationing, that's all. You didn't have to go and do that." His face was still tightened up with the pain. "I think you broke a rib."

"You're lucky I didn't break your goddamn head," I said. "Who is the fella you're sneaking around here looking for?"

"A little guy. Enderson, I think . . ."

"Eversen?"

"That's it. I saw him down the coast last week. He told me to come over and take a look at his skiff, to see if I could fix it up. I said I'd stop by sometime and see what I could do."

"If that's all you wanted, why didn't you come to the front door?"

"I was going to, I was going to!" he said. "I just came down the beach, is all. I looked in and saw you. I was just taking a closer look to make sure you weren't the guy."

"I think you're telling a goddam lie," I said. "You must be near-sighted. You stood outside that window a helluva lot longer than it took for you to see I wasn't your man."

"It's the truth, I'm telling ya! I didn't know who you were. I thought I had the wrong house. I was just making sure, that's all."

I let him go. "The more you talk, the fishier it sounds. You get the hell on away from here. If I catch you hanging around again, I'm going to break your goddamn neck."

I watched the guy take off down the beach, limping on the side where I'd caved him in.

I began to feel uneasy with all this action.

Back in the house, I put through a call to New York, to Lou Pulco's office. He wasn't in, but I was able to get his secretary at that private number.

"I'm sorry, Mr. Sorrell, but Mr. Pulco left late Saturday night for a four-day cruise on his private yacht."

"Hell, when I called yesterday you gave me some directives from Pulco," I said.

"I beg your pardon, Mr. Sorrell," she chirped up in offended tones, "but it is not strange for Mr. Pulco to leave directives in my hands which apply to situations many days in the future. Furthermore—"

"Then it must have been you and not Pulco who sent the telegram."

"What telegram?"

"The one that contained the information you gave me over the phone yesterday," I said. "It was delivered to the Hollitop yesterday."

"I sent no telegram, Mr. Sorrell. It's possible that Mr. Pulco may have sent it to you himself."

"Yeah," I said, confused for a moment. "Yeah, I guess it is."

I put the receiver back.

Something wasn't smelling right. Yeah, sure, it all seemed right, but somebody was crossing the wires somewhere along the line. How could Pulco have sent the telegram if he was out on a cruise?

He probably had a wireless aboard his yacht and I imagine he could have wired the message in. Still . . .

My thoughts were interrupted by the loud jangling of the doorbell. I looked out and saw an express truck parked in the drive. A middle-aged, pot-bellied guy in a green monkey suit had a finger stuck in the bell slot.

I went over and let him in.

"Parcel post package for Mr. George Eversen," he said, picking a good-sized, plain-wrapped package up from the stoop.

"Eversen's not in," I said. "I'll take it."

"Can't," the guy told me. "He's supposed to sign for it."

"What the hell is it?"

"Mister, how do I know? I only drive the truck and dump the

bundles."

"Look," I said, "if you wanna come back later, all right. Eversen's not in right now."

"Come back?" he squeaked. "Look, mister, I come all the way from Alpena—forty-five miles, get me? It's the farthest I've been away from home in my whole life!"

"That's a shame," I said. "You'll just have to bring it back, unless you want me to sign for it."

He raised the package for me to read a small white sticker. "See that? It says 'Deliver to addressee.' It's insured, even. I can't hand the thing over to anybody but this George Eversen joker."

I started to close the door. "That's your tough luck, junior."

"Hey, wait a minute," he said, sticking a foot in. "Are you any kin to this George Eversen?"

"Yeah, I'm Phil, his brother."

His face brightened. "Well, that solves everything! All you have to do is sign for him . . . "

"Okay, give it here."

"Ahn, ahn," he said, shaking his head shrewdly. "This will have to be handled with tact. Now you and I know that the trip from Alpena out here is one helluva trip, and we also know that I came out here with the express purpose—express, get it?—of delivering a package to your brother George, who is, beyond a question of a doubt, expecting this very important package, right?"

"Ditto."

"So, solid. Now what I know that you don't know is that the checker is going to check the signatures to make sure they're signed for what they're supposed to be signed for. In other words—"

"You want me to forge my brother George's signature on the receipt slip," I said.

He coughed discreetly. "After a fashion, yes—with the knowledge, of course, that you are doing your brother George and myself one great big favor."

"I'm game," I said. "Give me your pencil."

I set the package next to the door after the fat guy had gone, but after a while I started getting curious. I went over and took a look at the thing.

It was kind of heavy and firmly packed in thick brown wrapping paper.

It was addressed to Eversen in what looked like black crayon. There were two datelines, one at Culver City two days previously and one stamped Alpena, at 10:30 the night before. The return address was a P. O. Box in the same town.

I started clicking suddenly like a Geiger counter. Could it be possible . . . ?

I didn't waste any time. I went back to the kitchen and found a sharp paring knife. I made short work of the strands binding the thing and it wasn't long before I had the wrapping off.

Inside were five boxes, four the size of corsage containers and the other big enough to set two large-sized portable radios in. All were plain brown, sturdy boxes.

My hands were trembling when I grabbed the first one, and I was thinking about the way the package was delivered, the Culver City and Alpena datelines, and Naida telling me everything would be bells by tonight.

I was stunned when I opened the first one. All it contained was a filmy black negligee, with matching panties and bra. The second box contained nothing but panties, all sizes and shapes, and seven which represented the days of the week.

I was working on the third box when Eversen came in.

He did something when he saw me with that stuff that I'd never have imagined he'd have the nerve to do—he tried to tear my head off! He was yelling and screaming like a madman, clawing at my face with both hands.

"Leave it alone!" he bellowed over me. "You have no right to touch it!"

I came out from under him laughing, but the little guy was stronger than I thought and almost broke my shoulder with an arm lock. I wiggled away from him and fell forward on top, his head between my hands, slamming the back of his skull against the floor.

That took all the fight out of him.

"All right, Sorrell," he said defeatedly. "Now you know. I should have known you'd find out."

I got up, but it wasn't much of a joke anymore, not the way he'd tried to yank my shoulder out by the socket.

"I should kick the hell out of you!" I said. "If there weren't enough queers to put up with in this goddamn mess, I have to have one almost tear my arm off!"

He looked at me strangely for a long time before he got up off the floor. Then he finally got to his knees and started packing the stuff away, his face blank.

I went over and poured myself another drink. "Don't think you're by yourself, Pops. You've got a psychosis that's a lot less taxing than the one Naida Torneau's got."

"Sorrell," he said behind me in a small voice, "I . . . I can't help it . . . It's something I'm obsessed with—women's underclothes."

"Well, hurry up and put that junk away. I wanna have a talk with you."

He left quickly for his bedroom. When he returned, his face seemed to have regained its color and he was even a bit jovial.

"I'm glad that's over," he said. "I feel assured that you'll keep this—this trouble of mine confidential."

"Forget it. I want the car tonight, probably for the last time. I've got a couple of dates."

He gave me the keys. "Keep it as long as you want. I'm not going anywhere."

"I caught some guy peeking in the window earlier this evening," I said. "He told me he'd come over to see you. He's a sailor on the S. S. Maribou. Know anything about him?"

"Why, yes, I ... I told him to bring me some West Indian coral the next time his ship made the trip. You know, for decorations and things."

I thought about what the guy had told me. "That's funny. He told me he'd come over to do some work on your skiff. He said you'd asked him over for that purpose."

"Oh, yes, I do remember mentioning it to him a week or so ago. It slipped my mind. Did he happen to leave the coral here?"

"He wasn't carrying anything, and I don't think he liked the reception I gave him. He may not come back any time soon."

"Oh, what a pity," Eversen said. "I did so want that coral."

"About that telegram you told me about yesterday—you said Markle picked it up?"

"Yes, that's the information five dollars bought from the desk clerk. Why? Is anything wrong?"

"No, I was just trying to confirm a suspicion. Naida Torneau knew about the telegram. She told me Markle had let her in on it. I think she and Markle are getting set to make off with that dough tonight, and I plan to be on hand."

"Make off?" Eversen said, surprised. "You mean they have the money?"

"I don't think so, but I believe they've got things set up to put the wheels in motion. Naida told me last night she expected to put her hands on that money tonight. She also told me where to find Harv Cassiday. It's my guess that she and Markle have things arranged for a fast cross, with me in the middle."

"What are you going to do, Sorrell?"

I shrugged. "I don't have anything definite planned yet. I'm going to see Cassiday, but not, as the lady thinks, to rub him out. Mr. Cassiday and I are just going to have a nice little talk." I looked at my watch. "It's just a little after seven. When I come back tonight, it may be in a rush. Be prepared for anything."

Eversen put a hand on my arm. "Sorrell, couldn't I—well, couldn't I go with you?"

"Don't worry, Pops," I said. "I'm not going to forget you, if I'm lucky enough to pick up that cash!"

"But I … I feel so useless just sitting around doing nothing."

"You can do something right now. Do you have a gun?"

"Why, yes, but it's a big gun, a Magnum. Haven't fired it in years."

"Go rustle it up," I said. "It just might see some action tonight."

Twenty

IT WAS GOOD AND DARK when I left Eversen's place, no stars at all. My timepiece said it was a little past 8:30.

I had the Magnum packed up under my belt. It was bulky and the big round cylinder cut into my waist, but I was satisfied with it. A test firing on the beach let me see what it could do, and I especially liked the quick pin action of the hammer. It was a cannon, but I just might need a cannon tonight.

MONDAY NIGHT IS A LAZY one in Hollisworth. The most important thing was that I didn't spot any coppers. I wasn't too worried about them, what with Pulco's telegram, but I still didn't want to take any chances with some trigger-happy punk.

Deacon Street is three blocks past the Civic Center. It's drab and broken down, but still fairly neat.

I circled the block twice before I saw the old folks' home Naida'd told me about. It was a converted four-family flat, with transoms and fire escapes on both sides.

The sign outside allowed that it was primarily for old people, but visitors were welcome.

I parked the car two blocks away and came back on the opposite side of the street. When the traffic thinned out and I was sure nobody was watching, I crossed over and went directly to the entrance. From the front I could see six or seven old people sitting around in what was supposed to be the lobby. A reception desk sat in the center, where a gray-haired little mama was hunched next to the register, reading a confession magazine.

She seemed surprised when I interrupted her and her false choppers made a condescending clack.

"Good evening, sir," she said, bowing toward me. "May I help you? We have some very fine accommodations. Are you a stranger to Hollisworth?"

"Yes, I am. I'm looking for a friend of mine. A Mr. Anderson."

"Oh, yes," she said amiably. "You mean that fine young gentleman on the second floor."

"Is he in now?"

She shook her head sadly. "You know, it's a shame that such a clean-cut, good-looking young man should confine himself the way Mr. Anderson does. He's always in. Has been ever since he checked in with us last week."

"What room is he in?"

"Room 211. I'll call right up and let him know you're coming."

"I wish you wouldn't," I said. "I'd like to surprise him."

"I don't know if I should," she said hesitantly. "Mr. Anderson left strict orders not to let anyone come up unless I first notified him."

"That's all right," I said assuringly. "Mr. Anderson'll be very glad you made this exception."

"Well . . . if you think it's all right . . ."

"I'm sure it is," I said.

"I guess it's all right, then. His is the third door from the end of the hall."

"Thanks."

I went up the padded stairway. All those old gaffers seemed to be watching me, their lives suddenly titillated by the arrival of a stranger.

The hallway on the second floor was dimly lighted, and I wondered how the grandpas and grandmas managed not to break their goddamn necks coming down the staircase.

When I got to Cassiday's room, I unloosened the Magnum and gave it a quick check.

There was no answer when I first knocked on the door. My second knock brought a rustle from the inside. I moved over to the side and knocked again.

"The door's opened," a voice said. "Come on in."

I put a hand on the knob and released the latch. The door swung open slowly. The inside of the room was pitch dark, except for a slight illumination from the slightly raised window facing the fire escape. It was too damn dark for me to make an ass and a target out of myself.

"Cassiday," I called. "Cassiday, this is Andy Sorrell. Put the rod away, I just want to talk with you."

"I haven't got a rod, Sorrell," the voice came. "Anyway, I don't have to kill you—you're as dead as I am."

There was something about the helpless remorse in his voice that made me believe him. I went all the way, shoving the Magnum back under my belt. It may have been a mistake, but I wanted to play it on the line, sensing that this guy had the answers to everything I wanted to know.

I silhouetted myself in the doorway, but only for a fraction of a second. I saw Cassiday outlined on the bed as I came in, propped up on a pillow with both hands behind his head.

"Hello, sucker," he said. "Shake hands with your brother."

I came over to the bed and got a close look at him. There was light enough to let me make out his gaunt features, the premature baldness of a small head. The body was long and angling, suggestive of death in its easy repose.

I could hear him laugh deeply. "Get yourself a chair, brother. Sit down while I tell you about the biggest double-cross in history."

I went over and shut the door. Next to the window, I found a lopsided easy chair.

"That's right," he chuckled from the bed. "Make your self at home, Sorrell. What I'm going to tell you will take some time."

"Why don't you get right to the point and tell me where the money is?" I said.

"The money?" He laughed again. "Brother, I don't know where

that money is and I don't give a damn. That money's cost too much. That's the dirtiest money in the world!"

"Dirt is something that's never bothered me too much," I said. "For a half million bucks I'd gladly be the dirtiest guy in the world."

"And the deadest," Cassiday added. "Let me tell you how all this stuff got started, sucker, and maybe you'll understand."

"I'm listening."

"Where do I begin?" he said ruminatively. "At the heist? No, before that, when Benedict, Horvat and I were contacted by this wheel, this connection. That's how it got started. You see, we didn't even know each other before the heist. But the connect knew us—he knew us well. We'd been spotted months before. When he came to us with the prop, he knew just how we'd react. Fifty grand each, that's what he told us. No complications, no nothing. Just like clockwork, he said."

"What the connect didn't tell you was that the heist was private property," I said.

"Oh, sure, he was careful not to say anything about that. But it didn't make too much difference even after we found out. That fifty grand dangling in front of our noses knocked the hell out of all that."

"So you took off the bank," I said.

"Just like clockwork," Cassiday assented. "One fine Wednesday a few months ago, three smooth operating suckers took off that Jersey bank for five hundred thousand dollars. Our plan was followed right down to the letter. We crossed over to New York in a panel truck, where we met the connect and turned the cash over to him. Two months ago we were all supposed to meet up here in Hollisworth for the split, but our connect said we had to wait a little longer. He said he had to wait until things got cooler." He began laughing again. "We didn't know he was arranging to have us bumped."

"Have you bumped?"

"Sure, sucker! Didn't you know that you were a part of the plan? You were supposed to wipe out a hundred and fifty grand debt. Our man dropped the necessary information to the right people, and all he had to do was sit back and let you take care of us. But something went wrong along the way, Sorrell. You weren't taking care of the job fast enough. After you knocked off Benedict, Horvat and I saw what our pal was trying to do. Horvat wanted to spill, and he thought the best person to spill to was you, since you were out to get us. He rang our friend up and told him what he was doing to do if he didn't come across, and fast."

"Then it was your connect who fed Horvat the poison," I said. "But what was it with Lilly? Why did Lilly have to be eliminated?"

"Lilly got greedy and ambitious," he went on. "He's been fronting for this guy for years, you know, and he always got the short end. He found out about the caper and threatened to let the syndicate in if Big Boy didn't come through with the grease. He was a hazard that had to be erased."

I turned the things over in my mind, slotting them all in their proper positions. "Why did this guy try to kill Meg Inglander? What danger was she to him?"

"Meg was an afterthought," he said musingly. "He thought Horvat might have told her about the job. When you're playing around with half a million bucks, you don't take a chance on anything."

"What I can't understand," I said, "is why the guy didn't bump me off when he had the chance. He certainly tried to up at the Inglander place. Yet, when I found Lilly, he was content to bust my head open and call the cops. He could have wiped me if he'd wanted to."

"Use your head, Sorrell. It'd look a little strange if the coppers found you laid out with a slug in you and Lilly dead of poisoning, wouldn't it? Uhn, uhn, Big Boy took a chance leaving you. When you got away, he saw he could still use you as a diversion. And since he knew I was in town, he needed you to get rid of me when the time came. Oh, don't fail to keep your guard up, Sorrell—he plans to get rid of you at the right time, too."

"This guy doesn't know he's about to be double-crossed himself, does he? Naida Torneau talks about the dough as though it's already part of the family."

Cassiday grunted with interest. "That ought to be one for the books, sucker, but don't plan on being around to see anything like it go off."

"I'll only need to know one thing to make that possible," I said.

"Yeah." He chuckled to himself. "The name of the connect."

"That's it."

"Well, Jesus," he laughed at me, "don't you have any idea who he is? He's the syndicate's terminal here in Hollisworth, the guy with the most to say about everything. He was one of the two guys who double-crossed the syndicate."

"Two guys?"

"Oh, yeah, that's the surprise! See, I figured it out all by myself. My connect didn't just happen to think of that caper in Jersey. He had inside help, and lots of it. It's just not something you can think up in Hollisworth and engineer a couple of thousand miles away . . ."

That's when the crash came. The window sprayed over everything where I sat, slashing the interior with a wide sheath of glass. A heater bellowed twice and flame-hot next to my shoulder. I heeled around quickly out of the chair, going for the floor. I clawed the Magnum out and held it in a working position next to my side. The big hollow mouth cursed twice with a deep-throated hoarseness, making the whole room tremble with the passage of sound waves. Pieces of the wooden window frame disappeared easily. When I got over to the window, I could see my guy making the alleyway on the street side of the building.

I leveled the Magnum at the vanishing shadow and let it ram out two lead-nosed cousins. A scream sounded when my hearing came back, but I couldn't swear it was anything other than a mortally wounded cat.

Out on the street a car screamed past the mouth of the alley.

It was a black Thunderbird.

When I got over to Cassiday and took a good look, I could see two round spots, one to the left of his forehead and the other under the right cheek. It looked like somebody had taken a big red thumb and stuck it in.

By this time, the hallway outside had begun to mutter and I could hear some old dame screaming. I buckled the gun again and got out on the fire escape fast. The alley looked clear when I got to the ground, but I could see people gathering out front. I kicked off down the alley, trying to remember the exact spot I'd left the car in. There was a diagonal passageway that led out to the next street at the end of the alley. It was the only way to go, the quickest way to the car.

I trotted down to the end of it as fast as I could, unmindful of the dark patches. Just as I got to the end, a guy stood around in front of me and I could see he held a great big gun in his hand. I stopped abruptly and the guy held the gun shoulder high.

"You know, I'd just love to kill you," he said sweetly.

It was Hendricks.

Twenty-one

"Not as much as I'd like to kill you," I said.

He weaseled a hand underneath my coat and pulled out the Magnum. "It sure was nice of that lady to call up and let us know you'd be here tonight, wasn't it? Come on, let's go, big boy."

He shoved me over to the Buick parked at the curb. The same copper I'd blown in was behind the wheel.

"Your time's run out, Sorrell," Hendricks said. "You know what we've gotta do?"

"Don't keep me guessing."

He pushed me into the back seat and got in, giving the driver a signal to move on. "You're gonna die, comedian, that's what you're gonna do," he said, goosing me in the side with his rod. "All we have to do is make you."

"I don't wanna dance without you, daughter. Why don't we start head-up? All I need you to do is get the hell out of the way."

"That's the trouble right now, Sorrell—you're the one who's in the way."

"Sure, I've been the spur in somebody's ass. Why don't we start again," I said, "take a rounder route home. If it hadn't been for me you guys might never have believed there was any chance to slip your fingers around that half million."

He sneered. "Who needs you, comedian?"

"You do, straw boy. I know where that dough is and you don't."

The bluff was weak but it struck home. "If you know so much, where is it?"

"I'd be the most brilliant guy in the world if I told you, wouldn't

I, stupid."

"Maybe you'd be smart," he said meaningfully.

"That's what I'm being. If I let my insurance lapse in the face of a .45 I'd be a goddamn fool."

"You haven't been keeping up the premiums, Sorrell. Vin is picking up that money tonight. He's probably back at the office with it now. We don't need you for anything."

"Vin thinks he's going to pick that dough up," I bulled on. "The only payoff he's going to get will come from the business end of a rod in motion."

"You talk real good, Sorrell. The only trouble is, it's not going to get you anywhere. Vin says it's time for us to make a gift, because the Inglander family is raising a lot of hell."

"And I'm it . . ."

"With ribbons on," he said. "I wouldn't guess at it, but I'd say Harv Cassiday is laying up there in that room with a couple of slugs in him."

"What difference does it make? I was sent out here for just that reason—only it wasn't me who gave him the shove. Somebody fired through the window up there, and I came back with a few of my own."

"You understand that I don't really wanna do this," he said consolingly. "You've just gotta go, that's all there is to it."

"You'd rather eat dynamite than touch me," I said. "Didn't you read that telegram from Pulco? He gave me the go-ahead signal; nobody's gonna interfere with his okay."

"What telegram?"

"The one Markle picked up over at the hotel. Pulco left orders for me to carry on the assignment."

Hendricks began laughing. "If this is a trick, it's sure working the wrong way!"

"What the hell are you talking about, copper? Markle picked that telegram up yesterday. I called New York myself and found out about the orders even before the telegram got here."

"Somebody's pulling your leg," he said. "Vin didn't pick up any telegram for you."

"You're crazy! Markle even told Naida Torneau what the damn thing said."

"Listen, Sorrell, I'm not in the mood to argue with you. What the hell difference does a telegram mean to you now? You won't ever have to worry about anything like that again."

It might not bother me again, but it was bothering the hell out of me right then. Eversen and Naida had both told me about the contents of the telegram. New York had given me the same message. My first thought was that the hotel message could have been a phony, but I couldn't see how it could jibe all the way around.

I noticed we had come a good way out of town. The driver took a beach road. Deserted beach cabins strung themselves out next to the sea.

A mile or so further, we stopped in front of one of the joints. Hendricks made me get out while the driver stayed in the car.

"This is it, Sorrell," he said, grinning. "This is where we shot you down tonight. You were hiding out in this place."

"I don't like the goddamn place," I said. "I wouldn't feel right dying out here."

"Now isn't that just too bad?" Hendricks said.

I didn't rush the thing up any. I tried to take it as slow as I could. Hendricks prodded me up on the porch and through the front door. It was almost black inside, stinking with disuse.

I was grabbing at anything. This scene was sudden death and I had to goof up the script, or else.

Directly ahead of us was a table. Hendricks shoved me over toward the center of the room. When I got over to the table, I stretched my arms out behind me, coiling myself for one last try at that bastard.

My hands touched something long and heavy. It felt like a rod for hanging drapes. My fingers even felt the catch in the thing.

Hendricks was just raising the gun when I shot that rod around. It hit him right above the wrist, snapping the gun over in a corner. He bent over in pain, sucking in wind for that scream I knew had to come.

I raised the rod and brought it down as hard as I could right in the center of his head. His hat sprang off and I could hear the bone popping loose in his skull. He looked up at me with a wild-eyed silly expression and said, "Ow!" as though he'd just found out what was going on. He didn't even fall, he just froze there.

Then I went crazy. I raised the rod again and slapped it down just over his right eye. His neck jerked back with the force of the blow and I could feel the bone and cartilage pulling away from itself inside his head.

He melted all of a sudden, and I stood over him. I gave him two more good ones, then the blood started to get all over everything.

There was no way for him to live after I got through.

I got down and went through him till I found my gun, then I moved over to the door.

The guy outside couldn't see me, but I could see he was getting nervous wondering why he didn't hear a shot. He got out of the car pretty soon and unholstered his gun.

I didn't even bother with him. I pointed the Magnum at him and let it work out a single. The guy stopped in his tracks, suddenly lifted into the air by the invisible momentum. He crashed over against the Buick and got watery all the way down to his bones.

I ran over and got his heater, since the Magnum only had one more shell, then I got up under the wheel and started moving like hell out of there. When the police ever got to nosing around that place, I'd better be as rare as platinum.

In a burst of genius, I pointed the Buick around toward the police station. Yeah, sure, I know it sounds crazy, but I had to get my hands on Markle and that money before things blew up in my face. The black Thunderbird and the helpful little lady who got in touch with Hendricks told me that my time was measured in minutes.

I remembered the way I'd been brought into the station on my visits. It wouldn't be too hard if I kept right on upstairs, and I didn't expect any of those coppers would be looking for me to turn up right under their noses. If I was recognized, I'd have the advantage of surprise. I probably could scare my way out of there.

Right now I didn't think any plan was too dangerous. With Cassiday dead, the individuals who had taken the fatal trip down that five hundred thousand dollar primrose path had risen to four, not including my last two credits.

What seemed strange was that I'd only been accountable for fifty per cent of them.

Twenty-two

A FEW COPS WERE PLAYING ping pong, while several others stood gassing off at the desk in the back.

I came in the side door and went up the stairs to the second floor unnoticed. I didn't hesitate at Markle's door. I went right in—right into the barrel of a gun.

"Come on in, muscleman," said Tina Meadows.

I'd had a hand on my heater, but the electric fire burning in her eyes warned me against any damn stupid trick.

"Close the door," she ordered shortly. I came in and did as I was told.

She moved away from me, got out of reach. "I didn't expect to see you again, muscleman. I was hoping they'd bump you off quick." Her face knotted painfully, remembering.

"I've got a charmed life," I said. "I'm a man with a goal."

She went over to Markle's desk and picked up a couple of papers. "So's Vin. He'll be glad I kept you around when he gets here."

I grinned at her. "We're both contending for the crown of this year's biggest sucker, I see. I don't think Markle's going to be coming back anytime soon tonight—or ever."

"What are you talking about?"

"A good friend of yours," I suggested. "The one who was supposed to put you on Money Street. She and Markle have plans which don't include you."

She jerked the gun up at me. "You're lying! Vin's got all he needs to get the money. Naida never knew how to get it."

"I just met Hendricks a few minutes ago," I said. "He let me in on the whole story. Naida's been coming up here to talk with Markle."

"What does that prove?" she said sharply.

"It proves by that look on your face that you didn't know a damn thing about it. Naida and Vin never intended to give you a fair shake on that money. You're stranded, sweetheart. You'll be waiting here forever on Vin Markle."

"You're lying!" she hissed, coming around the desk. "Look at these papers! Vin picked them up in the room where you killed Brace Lilly."

I took the things. "What are they? They look official, all right, but not green enough to be the government issue I'm looking for."

"They're a bill of sale and a land deed for Lilly's," she said. I read the papers. "Lilly didn't own the club?"

"That's what those papers say. They say Lilly was only a front for the club, he only worked there . . ."

I could feel myself getting hot all over. My square block of a brain popped out of the formaldehyde for a minute and took a deep breath.

Why I didn't see it before, I don't know. Everything fitted right in, that's why Cassiday had laughed at me when he asked me if I didn't already know who the connect was.

It was funny, so goddamn funny I wanted to cry. "So Vin found out?" I said.

"Everybody thought Lilly was the syndicate's head here in Hollisworth," she said. "The real head is the one who has the money, and that's where Vin's gone. When he gets that money, he'll be right back, I just know he will."

"Don't hold your breath," I said, and at the same time I struck her one with the hand I held the papers in. It was like Hendricks all over again. The gun bounced over in a corner, and before she could make a go for it I put a choker on her pretty throat and threw her on one of the oversized sectionals, where she bounced a couple of times with a fine display of well-packed under drawers. I started for her again, but she cowered back, nylon thighs exposed temptingly.

"Sorrell . . ."

"Shut up," I said. "If you don't wanna die, keep your mouth shut until I get out of here."

I ran down the steps and around to the side door at the end of the staircase. Tina began yelling upstairs, but I wasn't worried about it. I was like a boulder rolling madly downhill.

Nothing could stop me now until I struck bottom.

Twenty-three

THERE WAS A LIGHT IN the study when I got over to Lilly's beach house.

The front door was standing wide open. I came in with the Magnum out, my finger tightened up on the trigger.

He was standing over the bodies when I got to the open doorway of the room off the hallway. There was a gun on the floor between them and the rug was littered sparsely with hundred dollar bills.

Eversen looked up at me sadly. "They were fighting when I got here, Sorrell. I heard the shots when I came through the front door. I guess it was about the money."

"I'm sure it was about the money," I said. "You make pretty good time on foot, or did you use the Thunderbird?"

He purposely ignored the question. "All this has been terrible! So many people have died because of that money."

I kept the Magnum pointed at his belly. "I don't think it's quite over, Pops."

He turned away from me. "I've got to have a drink. All this is a horrible shock!" He began to mix it at the liquor cabinet. "How about you, Sorrell?"

"Rye," I said. I didn't lower the gun.

He finished and brought a tall tumbler over to me. He'd put something in it to kill the smell of hand lotion, but I got a good whiff of it, anyway.

"Shouldn't we get out of here, Sorrell? The police—they'll probably be here soon."

"I don't think so." I handed the drink back to him. "I want to conduct a little experiment first. I want you to drink this."

He paled. "Drink . . . ? But, Sorrell, I don't like rye."

"I don't give a damn if you don't. I want you to drink this and I don't want you to stop until every last drop of it is gone."

He didn't take it.

"What's the matter?" I said. "Can't take your own medicine? I should have known about this crap when I caught the sailor hanging around your place, as much as I know about ships. What you do, buy it from him? Hydrocyanic acid is used to kill rats on ships. It also kills the hell out of people."

He watched me calmly and I could see the facade dropping off.

I looked down at Vin Markle and Naida. "Were they dead or alive when you killed Cassiday?"

He went over and placed the hot drink on the liquor cabinet casually. "I found them here together after I came back—yes, I'd borrowed the car from Naida. Evidently, she forgot that I had my own key. I heard them talking. I couldn't very well let them go through with their plans, could I?"

"At first she was only going to use Markle to strong arm the money out of you," I said, "but he had to be taken in as a partner when he found that bill of sale listing you as the bona fide owner of Lilly's. Markle put two and two together. You were the big man in Hollisworth, a secret well kept by Lilly and Naida."

"I have you to thank for letting me in on Naida's little scheme," he said easily. "She and I were going away together, or so I thought. I was to pay Markle off gratis . . ."

"And you found out they wanted all the dough."

"Precisely. However, I didn't see things quite their way."

"You have me to thank for letting you in on a lot of things," I said. "The night I went up to the Inglander place, I had a talk with you. You beat it up there and did Horvat in with your potion, since you'd already talked with him and he told you he was going to squeal to me. I should have known when you told me in a later conversation about what went on while I was on the premises. You described the shooting and mentioned that Horvat'd been poisoned. Nobody but the killer could have known so much."

He smiled. "Strangely enough, you didn't see the relation. I'm not exactly what you'd call a professional, like yourself. Horvat was going to shoot his mouth off, not only to you . . ."

"You slipped up again when you tried to incriminate Lilly. You told me Lilly'd had his face chewed up that night. The last time I saw Lilly, his face was as smooth as a baby's butt. I didn't get the drift then, either. Neither did I pick up when I had a talk with Naida. She had been expecting me to come up, because you had called and told her to expect me. You two have been working together ever since she came to me with that tip about Horvat. You also told her to give me that lead on Cassiday, but I told you I wanted only to talk to him, so you followed me over to his place and put the gag on him before he had a chance to tell me who the hell you were. You were taking your biggest chance then, because you had Naida call up the coppers. It had to be split-second timing: Kill Cassiday, get the hell away and leave me sitting on the scene."

Eversen was unperturbed. He went to his breast pocket, pulled out a cigarette and lighted it. "You make a better detective than an exterminator, Sorrell. There's only one thing—you don't know where that money is. How much do you want to get out of my hair?"

"Not much," I said. "Just all of it."

He laughed. "You'll never put your hands on that money without me."

"I think I can. I've been putting two and two together myself, Pops. Remember that package you got today? Unless I'm mistaken as hell, I'd say the cash was in it somewhere. That's the only part I can't figure out, but I know I'm right."

His bottom lip trembled nervously. "Don't be a fool! You saw what was in that package—"

"And I even gave you an alibi for it. Now I know why you gave me so goddamn much trouble about the package. Why, you even told me in so many words that the jig was up—you thought I'd found the money! When I labeled you a pantie freak, that was right up your alley. But I've been doing a lot of thinking about that package," I went on. "It went through too many changes to come from Culver City out here, too many precautions. Why so many flip-flops for a gross of panties? No, I think we'll just go over to your place and have a good look at what's inside."

He dropped his cigarette on the floor and crushed it out with the heel of his shoe. "Let's not be children about this, Sorrell! We could both be rich. I'm willing to give you a reasonable share of the money."

"You don't have any choice," I said. "You're going to give me all of it. It's worth it for the knocks I've taken."

"I should have killed you when I had the chance!"

"Yeah, it might have made things a lot simpler. Right now, we're going to get over for that dough. If I have any trouble out of you, I'm going to enjoy kicking your ass off."

I made him drive Naida's car.

It didn't take us long to get over to his place, and my mouth was drooling by the time we got there. It seemed almost unbelievable that I was going to put my hands on that money at last.

Eversen lagged around when we got there, but I booted him a couple of times and he got to moving.

I marched him right back to his bedroom. "All right, get it," I said.

He didn't move.

I laid the Magnum across his cheek smartly, rocking loose a few teeth.

"Don't, don't, Sorrell! Don't hit me again!"

"Get that goddamn money, then!"

He got down on his knees and crawled under the bed. He had a suitcase when he came out.

"Open it," I said, snapping on the bedroom light.

He freed the catches and raised the lid. That money was the greenest thing I ever saw, all laid out neatly in crisp, new packages.

I looked at it until my stomach started bubbling. "Now I can see why you tackled me when you found me opening that package. The panties were just a front in case something like that happened."

"Sorrell . . ."

"Shut up. Lock that thing up and take it out to the front."

Eversen was just a little ahead of me when we came in.

The voice said, "All right, gentlemen, if you don't mind, I'll relieve you of that little item."

Three things I felt at once: the gun in my ribs, both the Magnum and the one under my belt being snatched away and the immediate recognition of who was doing all this.

"Hello, boss," I said, without turning around.

Who else could it be but Lou Pulco?

Twenty-four

"GOOD EVENING, SORRELL," HE ANSWERED in that smooth voice of his. "Shame you had to put yourself in such a strained situation."

"I'll never get over it," I said.

Lou went over and snapped on the light. He reminds you of John L. Lewis, but he's a helluva lot fatter and better dressed. The gun in his hand looked out of place, but I knew he wouldn't hesitate to use it.

"Now I understand about the telegram," I said. "Eversen lied when he told me I'd received a telegram from you. It makes sense that he had to find out the same way I did, directly from your office. Your order fitted in perfectly with his plans."

Lou's big belly bubbled with a grim laugh. "My friend Eversen turned out to be a bigger fool than I thought. How he ever expected to double-cross me, I don't know."

Eversen raised his hands helplessly. "Lou . . ."

"No lies," Pulco said, waving him back with the barrel of his gun. "I knew something was going wrong when Vin Markle notified me that Horvat got tumbled with poison. Sorrell is not so subtle, you know. Then I contacted our man in Culver City and found that you had rushed delivery of the package by four days. I underestimated your nerve, Eversen. You, however, underestimated my perception."

Can you get any more stupid than me? Lou Pulco was the inside man with the syndicate, the fixer and chief of communiqués. He was one of the few people who could get a lead on the organization's plans.

"I know what you're thinking, Sorrell," he said, "and there're several people in New York thinking the same thing. I think things would be a good deal more healthier if l left the country indefinitely, the coast of South America, perhaps. That's why I brought the yacht, you see. Unfortunately, I'll be unable to take either of you with me. A regrettable circumstance, I must admit, but the only feasible one."

"But, Lou, I did what you wanted," Eversen whined. "The money—you've even got the money!"

"Please, spare me!" Pulco ordered. "Our scheme would have gone off smoothly, had you not interfered with Sorrell. Your eye was on the sparrow, was it not my friend? Five hundred thousand of them"

"But I had to, Lou! Sorrell was getting too close. Vin Markle and Naida Torneau—even Lilly—wanted to get in. I couldn't help it!"

"Let's not hash this thing out," Pulco said reprovingly. "It's a pity you had to start thinking for yourself."

He raised the gun deliberately and it cracked twice, three times. Eversen fell over on his face. The blood spread out quickly under him.

Pulco looked over at me. "Sorrell, I've always liked you, though you seemed a bit vacillating at times. Up till now, you've been able to handle all assignments I gave you. I imagine that your attention was distracted through no fault of your own this time, plus an irresponsible temptation. However, I can't permit you to tell anyone about what you've learned tonight. I also carelessly mentioned my destination. He raised the gun again. "Too bad, my friend . . ."

His shot was half good. I felt the bullet dig around my waistline, just over the kidney, the force of the bullet rocketing me against the wall. The pain blossomed and things got hazy red in front of my eyes. I did see him raise the gun again, but this time there was another explosion and I heard the lead plop into him.

He made a little squeak and dropped the gun, waddling as fast as he could for the doorway. When I looked toward the canted windows I could see Tina Meadows standing in front of a broken portion, screaming, her voice a jumble of wild words.

"You've killed Vin!" She screamed. "You bastards killed Vin!"

By this time, Pulco was hotfooting it out on the beach. I pulled up against the hot spot in my side and tried to ignore the rapid flow of blood. I started after that sonofabitch. It hurt like hell, but I wasn't going to let that fat bastard get away with anything, not as long as I had another ounce of strength.

I could barely make him out on the darkness of the beach, but he wasn't far ahead of me. He was snorting with the sudden exertion.

Down at the edge of the water, I saw a small motorboat with its nose in the sand. About two miles off shore Pulco's yacht bared its white side to the mainland.

He was pushing the boat out into the water when he saw me behind him. By the way he held his right arm, I knew Tina's bullet had got him there.

I'd forgotten he still had the Magnum and the police service pistol. He saw me balling down on him and raised the big gun and fired. I hit the sand just an instant before. He was cursing and snapping the trigger.

I got to him before he thought about the .38. I took him in my own time. I ducked as he tried to nail me with the butt of the gun and latched my fingers around his goddamn throat. He'd dropped the suitcase in the water, where it kicked around in the surf restlessly.

Pulco was infused with the strength of fear, but he couldn't get away from me. I felt monstrous with strength. I was killing him for everything that'd ever happened to me, all the way back to my old man, and it had almost a sexual goodness about it.

We struggled out in the water, him trying to get my fingers out of his gizzard. I didn't let him go. I held him until we were out where the water was about four feet or more, then I dragged him under, I dragged that sonofabitch under. His legs kicked up out of the water and he lost one of his shoes.

I was down in the water up to my neck, kneeling on the frantic whiplash of his good arm. The bubbles didn't come up long. I still held him after they stopped. I held him till I couldn't hold him any longer and the top of his head came to the surface.

Then I thought about the money, but the loss of blood didn't leave me anything to get myself moving with. I managed to wade up on the beach, but when I got there I saw the suitcase had broken open and the money was drifting out to sea, all of it! I scrambled after it, but I couldn't get any, not any of it! It seemed as though I could hear five hundred thousand voices laughing at me.

Then I began to laugh. I was crazy and I began to laugh. I wallowed around there in the water, laughing just like all those goddamn voices were laughing at me, like that goddamn voice in my head had been laughing at me for days.

I just sat there in the water and watched that money floating away, listening to the cry of police sirens, knowing they were only minutes away. I watched my money drift away from me, my money!

And I could see my old man coming across the sea to get me, walking on the water, just like Jesus . . .

Afterward

Clarence Cooper Jr.: An Appreciation

BACK WHEN I GREW UP on Flower Street in South Central, L.A., you didn't read then silly ass DC comic books, you read heavy duty Marvel. That was because their heroes suffered, strove to overcome obstacles. Those stories featured the likes of the blind Daredevil; the bullied Peter Parker—who was secretly Spider-Man; and the ever-pissed off, persecuted Hulk, subject to impulses he couldn't control.

Loyalty to these characters also had something to do with the fact that the Black Panther appeared alongside them in that now landmark issue of *Fantastic Four,* #52, in 1966, about a year after the Watts Riot. The Panther was not the first black superhero in comics, but T'Challa, the man under the mask, was one cool brother. Created by comic art pioneer Jack Kirby, the Black Panther was heir to the legendary Panther throne, benevolent ruler over the hidden, technologically advanced African kingdom of Wakanda.

You might ask what does all this have to do with Clarence Cooper Jr., a novelist from the streets of Detroit who in his notoriously brief career worked both ends of the literary spectrum. A writer with work compared on one hand to the stream-of-consciousness riffs of William S. Burroughs, author of *Naked Lunch*, and on the other to crime writers as varied as Jim Thompson and Mickey Spillane.

Just wait.

In my teen years, my reading tastes had broadened beyond comics.

I'd already been reading Poe and Conan Doyle's Sherlock Holmes stories, Richard Wright and even Agatha Christie. I then discovered the paperback originals of Robert Beck, aka Iceberg Slim, and his acolyte Donald Goines. Beck was an ex-pimp turned prolific pulp writer, and Goines, an admirer of Beck, had an education in crime, writing his first two books in prison after reading Beck's fictionalized autobiography, *Pimp*. These two wrote hard, terse books—with titles like *Airtight Willie and Me* and *Daddy Cool*—uncompromising novels that explored the black underworld. They wrote for Holloway House, a Los Angeles white-owned imprint with a background in soft-core skin mags. Back then you didn't find a Holloway House book in a bookstore, but on the spinner rack at the local drugstore, the corner newsstand, or in the bus station downtown.

Those racks were by that time also the home of Clarence Cooper Jr., whose brilliant, fiery, work defied easy classification: evoking raw street writers like Goines and Beck on one hand, Chester Himes on another. Shades of the classic crime novel conjoined with other literary forms, bringing to mind Baldwin and Malcom X (a childhood friend of Cooper's)—but informed, ultimately, by a yet darker, more fatalistic sensibility.

But earlier there had been the big leagues.

Cooper's debut novel, *The Scene,* had been published by a major New York house, Crown Books. It was the book that drew (and continues to draw) the most mainstream attention from literary critics. His wild talent, his ability with language, flashbacks and flash forwards, the intercutting of action and shifting points of view, all this was on display as he took the reader into a world of rollers and booster girls, drugs and whores, the Man, bogue and boo, doing so in a dialect so smacked-up that Crown, mindful of its white audience, felt a need to a put a glossary in the back. *The Scene* introduced us to Rudy Black—a kind of archetypal character for Cooper—a young ambitious man who don't give a damn, a character all about getting over as a drug lord.

The book put Cooper on the map.

For a brief run he was the shit. Then just as quickly, he fell from sight. His later work was pretty much ignored, especially the novel you're holding in your hands, published under the pseudonym of Robert Chestnut, less than a year later by Regency, a publisher out of Chicago that plowed similar acreage as Holloway House.

Like Goines and Beck after him, Cooper drew on his own funky life to tell his tales. He lived on the streets, and was in and out of prison. He wrestled with heroin and alcohol addiction all his life. Then in the late '70s—after an indeterminate stay at the 23rd Street YMCA in New York—Cooper was found dead on the street, with no money or identification. The hardcore reality of his life, the brute struggle for survival, is a truism that threads its way through his work.

The Syndicate is no exception in that regard, even though it's in many ways a very different kind of novel than Cooper's first. *The Syndicate* is a crime novel, one in a particular tradition, foreshadowing the amoral arena of Westlake's Parker books with a simultaneous backward nod to Hammett's *Red Harvest*. The main character, Andy Sorrell, is an enforcer, a fixer sent by a crime syndicate to reclaim swindled money.

In this book our first person narrator is white, or so I presume, though there are sideways riffs like ". . . or am I blushing," in which Cooper, whose color was probably unknown to the reader, seems to play with that assumption, if with nobody but himself. Whatever the case, Sorrell like many of Cooper's characters, comes from a world where you must be ruthless to survive. A man one step down, a hireling of others, struggling with an underlying anger and psycho-sexual hang-ups.

Just as it's hard as a contemporary reader not to think about race when reading this book—or about the savage violence against women—it's likewise hard not to think about the prejudices and perceptions about gays, common in the black community and just about everywhere in the late '50s. This was an attitude reflected in those X-rated Redd Foxx party records I'd sneak to listen to at my cracked bedroom door when I was a kid and my pops had a few of the fellas over for beer and dominoes. Cooper in *The Syndicate* was politically incorrect from the jump.

"I stood up, and all those sissies cringed when they actually saw how far I was up," says Sorrell in a sexual entendre that is as playful as it is vicious.

Not too long after that opening Sorrell beats a woman, a possible informant, a fatale who both attracts and repulses him. With her, he shows less restraint than with the gay hoodlums, bruising her up because she resembles his dead lover Carolyn — stirring his desires and his hate. In likewise savage fashion, Sorrell bulldozes his way toward the men he's been hired to find, the three doomed cats who made off with heist money intended for the syndicate.

This is another thing that strikes me up about this book: in terms of character and form, it plays like a reverse of *The Hunter* by Donald Westlake, aka Richard Stark. Except the influence, if there was any, goes the other way, as Cooper's novel was published two years before Westlake's. *The Hunter* marks the first appearance of the aforementioned Parker, a professional thief: a man almost purely Id, defined by his external actions. Westlake offers only the briefest of glimpses of his inner landscape over the course of the 24 novels he wrote about this remorseless hoodlum. In that first novel, Parker follows a straight line back to stolen syndicate money he himself had a hand in ripping off, only to be double-crossed by his partner. For Parker, killing is not pleasurable, but a necessary tool. A way to get what he wants. To remove an obstacle. To get back to the money. In *The Syndicate*, Sorrell too is following a straight line.

Like Parker, he goes from point A to point B by dint of will and ruthlessness. Sorrell too has no regard for others' lives. But unlike Parker, it might be argued Sorrell takes cruel pleasure in delivering his fatal sentences. Nothing is off the table when it comes to accomplishing his single-minded goal—or so it seems. For unlike the cold, emotionless Parker, Sorrell is heir to his perversions and greed. Sorrell finds himself coming apart at the seams, subject to impulses he can't control. For him, his .32 is not so much a weapon of utility. Rather a steel jacketed pacifier.

Sorrell is as different from Parker as he is from Chandler's moral crusader Philip Marlowe or Spillane's unabashed, narcissistic crypto-fascist Mike Hammer. Though he does share a certain warped sensibility with Goines' later creation, Larry Jackson, the hitman known as Daddy Cool.

Sorrell is a combination of vulnerability, self-destruction and inner rage, more akin to the sociopathic heroes of Jim Thompson who somehow—despite all common sense—maintain our interest and sympathies. Perhaps because we see in the dark recesses of our mutant souls some horrible similarity.

Cooper is a hard novelist to pigeonhole. His books share a certain commonality, but range across genre. *The Syndicate* is perhaps his most traditionally plotted crime novel. Others, like *Weed* and *The Farm*, remind one more of Goodis, in their noirish tone, books that deal with crime but don't follow the mechanisms of the genre. Then, of course, there's the free associative, multi-layered world of *The Scene*.

"My world man," Cooper wrote. "Yes, dopeys and drugman and dapper mocking Dans—the fuzz and pussy and pussy-collared: the *Jesus, please* extorters on cornerfront, in candy stores converted; the hurried, harried, hungry, for whom despair and life compose a litany—a dirge—preceding, yes, overlasting their damn-faced passing. Mine. And me. I'm them."

While *The Scene* was published in hardback in New York, most of his later output was published in Chicago, in pulp houses, first by Newsstand Library, and later by Regency, where now noted sci-fi writer Harlan Ellison was an in-house editor, and had a hand in publishing Cooper, along with Jim Thompson and Robert Sheckley. While the two apparently never met—Cooper was on and off the streets, and did much of his writing in jail—Ellison was proud of bringing Cooper's work to print, and thought of him as a "very literate, very troubled individual."

By the time *The Scene* hit the stands, Cooper was back in the joint doing a jolt. A few years before he'd done a sting at Michigan Reformatory at Iona from 1954-56. He wrote about the time in a piece for *Esquire*, published in 1961, explaining to its largely white audience the attraction some black folk, himself included, had to the separatist teachings of the Honorable Elijah Muhammad (nee Elijah Poole) who saw the white man as a devil—an interpretation you could take literally or figuratively, given how the white man bedevils the black.

Cooper encountered those teachings in the Michigan Reformatory, and spent a time after his release studying at the Detroit mosque. In the *Esquire* piece, he recounts the mythos underlying those teachings, a story involving Yakub, a renegade black scientist from an ancient, technologically advanced civilization of the Original Black Man (shades of Wakanda) who created the white race on an island off the coast of Asia—a devil race who would forestall the rise of the black race.

It was a story I'd heard in various forms over the years in the barber shop in my old neighborhood, along with tales about what brother got jacked up or shot by the cops out of 77th Division. Yakub's machinations brought to mind the High Evolutionary from Marvel Comics: a renegade scientist who did genetic tampering, crossing human and animals to create a new race of beings. It was like something out of a conspiracy theory broadcast by the likes of Alex Jones, a whack job firmly rooted in his own alt-reality. Cooper ultimately rejected the Nation of Islam, though at the same time understood its allure, seeing the Yakub rationale no more or less irrelevant to black people than that of the Christian church. "Maybe it's because being a black man, I've never quite believed in God, white or black." Indeed Cooper takes on the Black Muslims' Yakub fable in his novella *Not We Many*.

Cooper was an iconoclast, not an easy writer to categorize, to paint in corner.

He worked all ends of the literary spectrum.

No matter what form he was working, however, his work takes no prisoners. It is transgressive to the extreme. There is a dark fatalism, a mutant gene that haunts us all.

It seems no matter the material he tackled, though, he was bedeviled by the fact his work didn't receive more recognition. Cooper published five novels and a collection of novellas between 1960 and

67, and then stopped writing, disappearing, for all practical purposes, into the oblivion of the streets. He lost touch with editors, family, friends. In 1978, he was found dead on that NYC street, penniless and stripped of identification. He lay for months in the morgue, or so the story goes, before the police managed to notify his relatives in Detroit.

Gary Phillips

Biographical Notes

CLARENCE COOPER JR. PUBLISHED SIX books of crime fiction, all between 1960 and 1967. His novels and novellas have mostly to with the harder edges of life in black America: the underworld of the urban street, of drug addiction and violence. Cooper spent much of his life in that world himself, so biographical information is slim and anecdotal. We do know that he was born in Detroit in 1934 and later lived in Chicago, after having spent time in a Michigan reformatory. Sometime in the mid-1950s, while in his early twenties, he worked as an editor for *The Chicago Messenger*, a black newspaper, and reportedly began using heroin regularly at that time. His first book, *The Scene* (1960), draws from this autobiographical material. It was a critical success—regarded as an important novel, by a promising young talent—but his subsequent novels, though now well regarded, ended up in the slush pile at Regency House, a pulp publisher in Chicago, where they were brought to print by editor Harlan Ellison in the early sixties.

The Syndicate was also published in 1960, not too long after *The Scene*. A more straight forward crime novel, in a more traditional mode though no less transgressive, it appeared under the pseudonym of Robert Chestnut. Until now *The Syndicate* has not been published in the U.S. under Cooper's real name, but only abroad, where—with its pulp overtones and renegade violence— it is regarded as a cult classic.

Later books include *Weed* (1961), *The Dark Messenger* (1962), and *Black: Two Short Novels* (1962). His last book, *The Farm* (1967), was set in Lexington prison for drug addicts, a real-life institution originally known as the United State Narcotics Farm. *The Farm*, though published by a traditional New York house, was not widely reviewed in the literary columns and received a hostile reception from the black press.

Distressed and strung out on heroin, Cooper stopped writing shortly afterwards. He never shook his drug addiction, but died twelve years later in New York, in 1978, alone and strung out, on a street not far from his last known residence: the 23rd Street YMCA.

About Gary Phillips

SPECIAL THANKS TO GARY PHILLIPS, LOS ANGELES based novelist and editor, who wrote the afterward.

GARY PHILLIPS' NOVELS INCLUDE *The Jook, Warlord of Willow Ridge,* and a collection of three novellas in the Goines and Beck mold: *3 the Hard Way.* He has edited several anthologies, including the well-reviewed *The Obama Inheritance: Fifteen Stories of Conspiracy Noir.* Phillips is also co-editor of *Culprits*, a linked anthology that follows the fate of a heist crew post their swag-laden takedown.

More CRIME from Molotov Editions

From Edgar Award Winner Domenic Stansberry

THE WHITE DEVIL

NOIR THRILLER THAT WON THE HAMMETT PRIZE in 2017 for best crime fiction. Chilling story of a young American woman in Rome, an aspiring actress, who— together with her too charming brother—is implicated in a series of murders dating back to their childhood.

Stansberry nails the sultry, decadent, and erotically charged tone with one perfectly placed hammer stroke after another. Booklist.

THE CONFESSION

THIS PSYCHOLOGICAL THRILLER WON THE EDGAR for its portrayal of a Marin County forensic psychologist accused of murder. First published by Hard Case Crime, in 2004, as part of the neo-pulp renaissance, now regarded as a classic in contemporary crime fiction.

In the literary tradition of The Killer Inside Me, *and every bit as powerful. Stansberry is an extraordinarily evocative writer.* George Pelecanos, NY Times bestselling author.

In Translation

On Feeble Love & Bitter Lover: Dada Manifesto

TRISTAN TZARA, AUTHOR AND SABOTEUR, TRANSLATED now from the French by GILLIAN CONOLEY, with language further annihilated in celebration of the final assassination of dada, already dead, and in public edification, too, of the centennial of the movement's continual death, long and feeble crying, oh, you and your cash register, please note: Bar Code, true love, ambition, literary syphilis.

Limited edition translation / annihilation published on occasion of the Dada Worlds Fair, San Francisco, November, 2016.

Drama

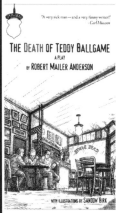

THE DEATH OF TEDDY BALLGAME
Robert Mailer Anderson

FROM THE BEST-SELLING AUTHOR OF *BOONVILLE*. A blackly comic two-act play. Quickly paced, sharply written political theater blending comedy, horror, and social satire in the tradition of the Grand Guignol. Action commences in a local café in San Francisco—post-911, post-Guantanamo, post-Apocalypse—when an unnamed catastrophe leaves the surviving patrons immersed in the erie glow of a world gone wrong.

A very sick man – and a very funny writer!- **Carl Hiaasen.**

About Molotov Edtions

WE ARE AN INDEPENDENT PUBLISHING HOUSE with an emphasis on crime fiction and other transgressive matter. Our books are available through bookstores, online retailers, and directly through our website. Visit us at www.molotoveditions.com to sign up for our newsletter and get news on our latest and forthcoming titles.

If you like our books, and bought them online, both our writers and editors would appreciate your comments in the place where they were purchased, or anywhere books are discussed.

www.molotoveditions.com.

Trade and Special Editons of *The Syndicate*

The Syndicate is available in two high quality, digital offset print editions from Molotov Editions. These include a limited release hard cover, the first 26 copies hand numbered, letters A-Z, available only through the publisher. For general release, there is a high-quality trade paper, initial press run of 500, printed at BookMobile. That first run and all subsequent printings will be available to the trade through Itasca Distribution— and to readers wherever books are sold. Quality print on demand and e-book editions will also be available.